Puffin Books

THE UNDERRUNNERS

Margaret Mahy is a New Zealander who has been writing stories from the age of seven. She writes for a wide age range, and has been awarded the Carnegie Medal twice and the Esther Glen Award three times. She lives near Christchurch, South Island, has two grown-up daughters, several cats, a large garden and thousands of books.

Underrunners

MARGARET MAHY

PUFFIN BOOKS

PUFFIN BOOKS

Published by the Penguin Group
Penguin Books Ltd, 27 Wrights Lane, London W8 5TZ, England
Penguin Books USA Inc., 375 Hudson Street, New York, New York 10014, USA
Penguin Books Australia Ltd, Ringwood, Victoria, Australia
Penguin Books Canada Ltd, 10 Alcorn Avenue, Toronto, Ontario, Canada M4V 3B2
Penguin Books (NZ) Ltd, 182–190 Wairau Road, Auckland 10, New Zealand

Penguin Books Ltd, Registered Offices: Harmondsworth, Middlesex, England

First published by Hamish Hamilton Ltd 1992
Published in Puffin Books 1994
1 3 5 7 9 10 8 6 4 2

A Vanessa Hamilton Book

Printed in England by Clays Ltd, St Ives plc
Filmset in Sabon

To Paula – a wonderful reader

CHAPTER ONE

―――― · ――――

As Tristram Catt and Sylvia Collins walked home from school, the driver of a yellow sports car, brighter than the soft autumn sunshine, braked sharply and slowed up beside them. A smiling man looked out. Thick grey hair tumbled on to his forehead, and dark glasses hid most of his face. He looked handsome and rich.

'Hey!' he cried cheerfully. 'You kids know your way around, don't you? Am I on the right road to the Children's Home?' He and his car seemed like creatures from an up-market galaxy, light-years beyond Gideon Bay.

'Straight ahead!' said Tris, pointing up the road. He stared yearningly at the car, thinking it was the most beautiful thing he had ever seen. It was a Lotus of some kind, an old one, but lovingly polished and looked after.

'There's a sign behind you,' said Sylvia. The man turned slowly, apparently noticing for the first time the yellow A.A. sign pointing ahead. *Feather-stonehaugh Children's Home*, it said. The man read the name and laughed to himself.

'It's hard to believe it's pronounced Fanshaw, isn't it?' he remarked.

'That's what everyone says,' Sylvia replied.

But the car was already moving on, leaving Tris behind, still walking with Sylvia. They watched the car round the corner before Sylvia started talking to Tris again. Using her bossiest voice, she repeated what she had been saying when they were interrupted.

'I'll walk home with you,' she repeated. 'I haven't ever seen inside your house.'

'Whoa back!' said a deep gritty voice inside Tris's head, bouncing back and forth somewhere between his eyes. *'She's spying!'*

'You can't!' Tris said quickly. 'Because of my dad working at home. We'd have to whisper and tiptoe.'

'Whisper and tiptoe!' boomed Sylvia. Tris could see the thought of a tiptoeing-whispering after-school life horrified her. 'Do you go round whispering and tiptoeing all afternoon?'

'There's never anything to eat,' prompted the gritty voice in Tris's head.

'Yes, I do. And there's never anything to eat,' Tris said. 'We never have any cake.'

Sylvia looked suspicious but uncertain. Though they were both eleven years old, she was taller and tougher than Tris. She spoke as if everyone around her were slightly deaf. Whenever he walked home with Sylvia and Sylvia's gate came in sight, Tris would cross the road, pretending he had seen something interesting on the other side. Once, Sylvia had seized him and tried to kiss him goodbye – 'just for practice,' she said. Tris suspected she had chosen to practise on him because he was small and she thought she could get a good grip on him. Tris had fought back, not wanting to be practised on by Sylvia. 'Hold still! Hold still!' she had bellowed at him. 'I only want to see what it's like! It'll be all over in a minute.' She had landed a kiss next to his ear and another on his eyebrow, knocking his glasses crooked before he had managed to get away.

'It's not so great!' Sylvia had said, shrugging and pulling a face. Then she strode away through the gum trees to her house on the hill, leaving Tris alone and shaken on the side of the road. Although she hadn't tried kissing him again, in the last day or two she had become curious to see where he lived, and determined to make him invite her home.

'Does that Mrs Emanuel whisper and tiptoe when she visits your father?' Sylvia asked as slyly as anyone with a booming voice could ask anything.

'It's different for grown-ups,' Tris answered.

'Everyone says she's out to *get* your father,' Sylvia cried as if they had several paddocks between them and not just a narrow road. 'My dad says he hasn't got a chance.'

It was Tris's turn to shrug his shoulders and turn away, but Sylvia hadn't finished with him yet.

'Don't you get lonely, living out there with no cake, and tiptoeing and whispering all afternoon?' she called after him.

'I'm used to it,' Tris called back.

He was never lonely these days. Even before they got to Sylvia's gate Tris would know Selsey Firebone was *with* him, moving as silently as only a trained outer-space, alien-detecting secret agent can move. Sometimes, Selsey Firebone seemed to be walking beside Tris, but mostly he walked *with* him, *through* him. The feet scuffling in the shingle on the side of the road wore Tris's sneakers or sandals, but they belonged to Selsey, too.

Mentioning cake brought on pangs of after-school hunger in Sylvia and she suddenly lost interest in Tris's foodless, whispering, tiptoeing house.

'Okay. See you tomorrow!' she said, and off she went, between the Australian gums planted on either side of the private road up Collins Hill.

'*Right!*' said the deep gritty voice, aloud now, slipping out between Tris's lips, though it was not his voice. The game of danger was starting again. Tris and Selsey were secret interplanetary agents, passing from galaxy to galaxy, through hidden timewarps, tunnels in the seventh dimension, moving under real life like ghosts, and keeping the world safe for civilization.

Of all the children at school, Tris Catt had the longest walk home. Some people were collected at the school gate – Elaine Partridge, for instance. Mrs Partridge was always waiting in her new blue Mitsubishi Lancer Liftback even though the Partridge house was only a mile away. After Elaine, with her white socks, and shining blonde plait of hair, had scrambled into the car, her mother would slam it through the gears and they would shoot away, leaving everyone else staring enviously after them. Tris, too, would stare enviously after the beautiful car, then set off with Sylvia Collins and the Morley twins along the road – Morley's Road – that skirted Collins Hill. Guy and Brian Morley did not walk (no Morley ever walked anywhere), but rode backwards and forwards on their ten-speed bikes, doing wheelies, and laughing and jeering at indignant dogs as they sped down again. Sometimes they were friendly, willing to let other people ride their bicycles, and sometimes all they wanted to do was torment Tris and Sylvia as they walked home. You could never tell which mood they would be in.

This part of the road was tarred and respectable. 'After all,' Sylvia sometimes said in a dark meaningful voice, 'Mr Morley was a councillor. Trust him to look after his own road first.' But the real reason for this road being so respectable was that it led past the Featherstonehaugh Children's Home. It was only after the Children's Home that the road grew rutted and patched with pot-holes.

After Guy and Brian had vanished between the neat lines of fruit trees in their father's orchard, after all danger of being kissed by Sylvia was behind him, Tris still had two small hills to climb. Plodding over the top of the first hill, he looked down and then out. There, almost under his feet – so that it seemed

5

as if he and Selsey Firebone could jet down into its chimneys – lay the great rambling house where the Featherstonehaugh family had once lived. Beyond the house and its well-grown trees, Gideon Bay nudged a sly elbow of water and mud into the land, and on the other side of that rippling muscle of water lay a long, brown, barren, brooding peninsula, a giant, diving towards the mouth of the bay, aiming at the open sea beyond. Tris always looked for this uncouth figure, back humped, shoulders twisted with inhuman muscles, steep sides eroded into ribs. The outstretched arms were welded into one powerful arm, but the weak fingerless hands dissolved into the sea. There, between those hands, you could see, if you knew where to look for it, a little grey box. The diving man was desperately holding treasure above the water, and looked, from where Tris stood, as if he were losing his grasp on it. The treasure that appeared to be sliding down a slope into the water was Tris's house.

Tris had begun walking to and from school after his mother had driven off in the family car, never to return. In those days, his father would walk halfway to meet him for something about the road had frightened Tris. He was still unable to explain just why the peaceful road, overgrown at its edges and dappled with afternoon light, had scared him so much. Of course, people expected boys who were small and thin and wore glasses to be slightly cowardly, but being small really meant that you had to try harder.

He had tried to take no notice of the pictures his mind kept on trying to show him ... pictures of some strange car (he could never be sure of the make) drawing up beside him, of a hairy arm scooping him in and carrying him away through a space-time wormhole and into an alien dimension.

Tris grinned, suddenly entertained by this old childish fear.

'*Good kid!*' said Selsey Firebone.

Beside the grey box that was Tris's home was an odd flicker – now red, now blue, now quite invisible – coming and going as he looked at it. His father had hoisted the family flag which he had sewn for Tris years earlier: a huge red cat on a blue background. It waved from headland to hilltop to beckon the traveller safely home. Tris nodded, pleased to see it, then plunged down the hill towards the fence of the Children's Home. Once at the bottom of the hill, he paused, looked right, looked left, then swerved off the road into the roadside scrub.

On the last part of the journey home Tris moved by two secret paths known only to him and to Selsey Firebone: one, along the fence of the Featherstonehaugh Children's Home, and the other through a deep ditch so overgrown with long grass that it made a sort of tunnel, running parallel to the road up the second hill almost as far as Tris's gate. Selsey Firebone dived and hid with him – an intergalactic secret agent, skilled in the eastern arts of kung fu and karate, as well as the mind-control skills of the Dwango Planetary system. Selsey could walk as quietly as a cat. He could box and wrestle, and fence with every kind of sword, besides being a dead shot with any rocket launcher. Wriggling along between the tall roadside scrub and the fence of the Featherstonehaugh Children's Home, Tris would speak first in his own voice, and then answer in the special deep, dark, gritty *hard* voice – a ruthless voice – Selsey Firebone's voice.

'They're after us, Selsey!' Tris's own voice was light and tense as he pushed along between the wire mesh and the manuka scrub, dense as a wall.

'*How many of them, Clint?*' Selsey asked. He called Tris by various gritty, sharp names, quite unlike his real name which always sounded to Tris himself like the call of a bird.

'Only five or six. Maybe seven!' he replied, narrowing his eyes. Selsey gave a little snort of laughter.

'*Seven! Ha! They'll learn.*' (Tris smiled for Selsey with his teeth closed). '*Of course, it'll be too late for them by then.*' And indeed seven enemies were nothing to Selsey and Tris together.

No one else used the track along the line of the fence. No one even suspected it was there. So it came as a great surprise to Tris, caught up in a skirmish with the Veng on the planet Mobilus, to find himself stepping on freshly turned earth. '*A trap,*' muttered Selsey Firebone. But the dirt had spilled through from the other side of the steel mesh. Someone had been digging in the Featherstonehaugh Children's Home shrubbery.

'*It looks like a grave,*' said Selsey Firebone, never alarmed by such ideas. '*The Matron's killed some kid, and they're burying him secretly.*' Twigs and leaves bulged through the diamond spaces made by the mesh. Someone had certainly been working there with a spade.

As Tris stared at the scraping under the fence, someone hidden behind the leaves gave a muffled sneeze. He jumped, just as he would have done if one of the Veng had snorted in his ear. The leaves rustled and parted and a face looked out – a smooth, olive-skinned face with shining eyes and a long mouth, grinning like the slot of a moneybox.

'Ta daaaah!' cried the face in a kind of whispered shout, as triumphantly as if it were making a grand announcement. Then it crumpled up and sneezed again. Within the blink of an eye Tris could see it was the face of a plain, knobbly girl with black hair clipped shorter than his own.

The unexpected face gave Tris the sort of fright most people get several times a day, nothing terrible, and all over in a second. However, along with this face came something very like a memory: a memory of patchwork . . . no . . . of patches . . . patches of dark rich colours displayed on a wall.

'Tristram Catt?' asked the girl.

'Who wants to know?' said Tris. The girl stared at him intently, her moneybox smile fading, her expression altering and becoming closed and secretive.

Feeling embarrassed because one of the Featherstonehaugh Children's Home kids must have listened to him talking to himself, Tris began to walk away. Then, feeling awkward and half sorry because he had been unfriendly, he turned to say something else. The girl had disappeared. All the same she must have been watching him through those leaves. Listening from those leaves she must have heard his stories and learned his name.

Tris walked stiffly to the end of his secret track, past the gates and past the big notice that read, *Featherstonehaugh Children's Home*. 'Fan-shaw! Fan-shaw!' he sang softly under his breath to show how carefree he was. When he reached the hidden ditch though, he began to scramble, and he scrambled under the curving plumes of grass until he burst out of the ditch almost in front of his own gate, his embarrassment left behind.

Tris checked the letter-box. Over the last year he had found himself hoping for, half expecting, a letter with his name on it, a letter with Australian stamps in the corner, showing that it came from his mother in Sydney. Usually, the letter-box was empty. But today there was a community newspaper, a colour brochure describing turtle-wax and special brushes you could buy to keep your car clean, and a card from the council addressed to his father, warning him to control the gorse that spread up from the creases in the sides of the peninsula.

Tris put the card, newspaper and brochure into

the schoolbag hanging from his shoulders, and was just about to open the gate, when he heard the sound of an approaching car struggling uphill behind him. It certainly wasn't the Lotus. All the same it sounded as if it were manned by aliens.

Tris pushed the gate wide and, without turning round, stood waiting while a battered green 1969 Volkswagen 1500 drove through, rattling its mud-guards and bonnet at him. The driver was Victoria Emanuel, the same Mrs Emanuel who Sylvia had said was out to get Tris's father. Her small daughter, Rosie, sat in a safety seat behind her. They stopped and waited for him, so Tris had no choice but to get in and drive with the aliens who, only recently, had begun a slow invasion of his lonely land.

CHAPTER TWO

—— · ——

'Hello there!' said the driver, Victoria Emanuel, as he scrambled into the car. 'What have you been up to today?'

'Nothing,' said Tris. 'Just school.'

She turned her head and their eyes met.

'You're giving me that sharp look again, Mr Ratty,' she said. Tris grinned and ducked his head a little.

'It comes out of my eyes before I can stop it,' he explained.

'You don't have to worry, Ratty,' Victoria said. 'I'm harmless.'

She did look harmless. She had fairish hair and crooked eyebrows but Tris thought she might be secretly changing his life without his permission.

She called him Ratty because a little while ago, when she first began visiting, she had decided that Tris had a grave, round face and small neat ears just like the water rat in *The Wind in the Willows*. 'All you need is the whiskers!' she had told him. 'You make a good Ratty!'

'Ratty!' shouted Rosie, Victoria's three-year-old

daughter, from the seat behind. She loved Tris and wanted him to look at her, so she hit him across the back of the head with a long, stretched-out knitted monkey called Bombom. Tris swung round, pulling an outer-space face at her. Rosie shrieked with pleasure, and clasped Bombom over her own face.

If Tris had been walking home he would probably have climbed on to the rocky spine of the peninsula and wandered along the ridge, up over the rise that he and his father called the Bum, down into the small of the diving giant's back, hairy with tussock and dead grasses, and then up again over the twisted shoulders. However, the Volkswagen had to stick to the roughly-graded road that wound in a great S shape in between the bottom and shoulders of the diving giant.

'Watch out,' Tris said sharply. 'Underrunners!'

A sly hole appeared in the road ahead of them.

'I know,' Victoria said, but Tris wanted to remind her. After all, this was his place, not hers.

There were many crumbling holes among the clumps of tussock. Tris knew them all. 'Tunnel erosion,' his father sometimes muttered, kicking gloomily at the grassy edges, while Tris imagined a whole network of secret passages running under his feet . . . shafts from other dimensions, tracks that the Veng could use. Winter swelled the earth with rain, summer dried and shrank it. The treacherous tunnels formed under the grass and tussock, occasionally eating their way to the surface.

'*Time-space worms nibbling at the world,*' said Selsey Firebone in his tough voice. Tris had hidden three tins of baked beans, four bottles of Coke, a packet of peanuts, a torch and a tin-opener at the back of one of these holes. '*Right!*' Selsey Firebone had muttered, scrambling out of the hole along with Tris, '*Now we've got a hiding place if the balloon goes up!*'

The car moved carefully forward. A new view opened on to a wide tidal bay, with the hills on the far side of the bay reflected exactly in the thin film of water lying over the sand and mud. The water gave the reflected slopes a glow that the real hills didn't have. If you could get to the other side of that glassy film you'd find the very place you started out from, but somehow enchanted.

'It's so romantic out here,' exclaimed Victoria with a sigh.

'People always think it's romantic,' Tris said, 'but they don't have to live here.'

After all, some people did not want romance.

'I'm sick to the back teeth with romance!' These were the last words Tris ever remembered hearing his mother say. They stuck in his memory like an advertising jingle ... once heard, never forgotten. '*Sick of romance, romance, romance! Sick of romance and gone!*'

One day, soon after saying this, she had packed her clothes and her tennis racquet and had disappeared.

'She ran away to find her fortune,' Randall Catt

would say lightly, but actually she had driven off in a blue Triumph Herald with a faulty distributor.

'She deserved more than that car. It was due for a complete recondition and valve regrind anyway,' Randall had said with a sigh.

Tris had missed her, though not in the way he had missed Dearie Tyrone, the baby-sitter who had looked after him while his mother went out to work when they had lived in the city. Though he could hardly remember what Dearie had looked like, he remembered her soft, cushiony hugs, and the lopsided cakes she made. He missed his mother differently, missed her because she *was* his mother and he was part of her, even if he had turned out to be a part that she didn't want. By now, the idea of having a mother was mixed up with the idea of having a car and of living in a house surrounded by big shady trees, with a tennis court out at the back. 'That's where the tennis court will be,' his father had once told Tris, gesturing at one of the few flattish areas of long grass, dry and harsh with summer heat. 'Of course, we won't be to able hit anything too hard.' Standing side by side they had looked out over the tawny slopes falling down to the sea, and had imagined tennis balls zooming off into space.

'Everything dies here. Even Tristram's stunted,' Tris's mother had cried, calling him Tristram as if she didn't know him very well. She had worked as a land agent from when he was three months old. It was Dearie Tyrone who had fed him and played

15

games with him and hugged him, too, along with her own children, Tod, Damon, and wild, shaggy Cecily, his protector when Damon was in an unkind mood. Tris remembered his mother's words, but not her voice. He remembered Dearie's voice, but nothing she had actually said.

The road sloped down and then ended. There was no gate. The Catts' house rose up out of the slope of tussocky, dry summer grass. It was what was called a pole-house, built on a platform which hung out over the slope on great poles, driven deep into the rocks and stones of the peninsula. A curious mixture of garden and rubbish heap spread out around it: buckets with broken handles, beds of marigolds, late lettuces, a bath with clawed feet, a pump, a trellis covered with dead beans, a collection of battered garden tools, spare tyres (for the car they did not have but might have again some day), a chopping block and an axe, surrounded by chips of wood, a motorbike that did not go any more, and tins saved to be recycled as pots for plants. The flag with the blue cat on it snapped proudly over this strange collection of things.

As Victoria turned to pick Rosie out of the safety seat in the back, Tris raced in ahead of her, anxious to tidy up. If she came in and saw too much disorder she might begin tidying it up, and his father would be so grateful that Victoria would be sure to *get* him.

Tris slammed the door just to make sure Randall knew he was home. He looked round the big room, the main room of the house, in despair. There was his bed, unmade still, in its little alcove, surrounded with glossy posters advertising wonderful cars ... Alfa Romeo, Ferrari, Mercedes. His pyjamas lay on the floor with a patchy black-and-white cat called Puzzle curled up asleep on them.

'How you going, sport?' Randall yelled immediately, but he didn't come out from the tiny office where he sat with his drawing board, designing gardens and tennis courts for other, richer people.

'Fine! Sort of!' Tris answered, dropping his pack on the floor and skittering to and fro. He snatched up his pyjamas so suddenly that Puzzle rose into the air and flipped over like a pancake. Tris crammed them under his pillow, dragging the quilt over his lumpy bed. Then he rushed wildly to mop up the small pool of water that often lay in front of the refrigerator, which ran on kerosene. 'Dad, why don't we have electricity brought out here?' He already knew the answer but felt compelled to ask every so often.

'I've told you! We can't afford it,' Randall shouted back. 'It would cost thousands of dollars, and anyway I hate the look of power lines.'

Their second cat, Fat Tab, was asleep on the table, a little skirt of tabby fur fluffed out around him. Tris flicked him with the wet dishcloth and he leaped away, his ears sloping back irritably. As he leaped, he knocked over the car-fund moneybox, which always seemed to be a little on the light side.

'Tris, could you do your old man a favour?' called Randall.

Tris knew he wanted a cup of coffee.

'Too much coffee's not good for you,' he shouted back, piling dirty dishes into the sink. 'It damages your DNA.'

It was Brian Morley who had told him how dangerous coffee was.

'It damages your DNA,' Brian had said, inching along as slowly as he possibly could on his ten-speed. 'It was in Wednesday's paper.' Brian loved gruesome things, though he had to find them in the paper since he was not allowed books about violence at home.

The table was covered with dusty paw marks, large and small. Both cats, the thin one and the fat one, had obviously been checking it out for food. Tris began wiping the table top, sweeping his arm backwards and forwards like a windscreen wiper across a car window, looking anxiously around the floor as he did so for any signs that the hens might have been inside. No one would know he was wiping the table with the same cloth he had just used for mopping the floor.

'It'll damage your DNA if I don't have a cup of coffee . . . I'll become one of the powers of darkness,' Randall cried, making a cackling, vampire noise from the little room. 'I can feel the change coming on now.'

Tris draped a tea towel, clean but unironed, over

18

the dirty dishes in the sink. He could see dust on his plastic dinosaur collection and on the case of Randall's binoculars, standing beside the green gorgosaurus. But it was too late to do any dusting – Victoria and Rosie were already crossing that part of the pole-house platform which served as a veranda. Tris was sure Victoria would notice the two plastic buckets by the glass doors. One was filled with ashes and scraps for the compost heap, the other with scraps for the hens who had already checked the buckets, pulling old bread and wilted lettuce leaves on to the door mat. Victoria stepped over this mess, opening the big glass doors that almost, but not quite, matched each other. Rosie dashed in as if she were coming home. Randall had bought the glass doors separately from two different demolition sites.

'Who's that?' he called anxiously, hearing footsteps.

'Me!' said Victoria. 'I made a batch of Anzac biscuits, but there are too many for Rosie and me to eat on our own.'

If ever there was a way of *getting* Randall it would be to bake him Anzac biscuits, thought Tris.

There was the sound of a chair being pushed back. The door opened. Randall came out. He was a short, thin man, and although his mouse-coloured hair was retreating around his forehead and at his temples, he wore it long at the back, tied into a scraggly ponytail. He had mild blue eyes with long dark lashes, just as beautiful as any film star's, and was the opposite of Selsey Firebone in nearly every way. Selsey was always ready for anything; Randall never was. Selsey synchronized his watch with Greenwich Mean Time; Randall forgot to wind his watch and often thought it was yesterday. Selsey was tall and silent and strong, moving like a shadow, ready to take on the Veng at a moment's notice. Randall wore old tennis shoes, and if invaders came, he was quite likely to invite them in and try to counsel them. He had once worked with the Armed Offenders' Squad, but only because for years he had been part of a Samaritan Group Centre, counselling fathers with a history of violence.

'Have you ever thought of taking an anger-management course?' Tris had heard him saying on their radio phone to someone only last week. His real work, the work that earned money, was garden design, which was how he had come to meet Victoria, who was a part-time gardener, as well as a widow.

'Anzac biscuits!' Randall cried. 'A party!'

Tris pulled a face to himself.

'I'm just going to take Bessie some water,' he said. Bessie was the nanny goat. Her responsibility was keeping the gorse and broom down, but it was hard work for one goat, particularly when she had to be chained up so that she wouldn't eat the young trees, which she greatly preferred. 'Could I take her an Anzac biscuit, too?' Tris asked.

'These biscuits are for people, not goats,' said

Randall, but Victoria laughed and pushed two biscuits over towards him. Tris rescued some crusts from the hens' bucket, then picked up another bucket for the goat and made for the door.

It was a long time since there had been any rain. The water in the tanks under the house was low. Tris waited patiently for the slow trickle to fill the goat bucket. From here, the Featherstonehaugh Children's Home looked like a mysterious inn in a horror film, a place whose heavy front door would be opened creakingly by a butler seven feet high, with a scarred face and a bolt in his neck.

'*Not to worry,*' said Selsey Firebone. '*We're more than a match for them.*' He didn't say for whom. It could have been Guy and Brian Morley in certain moods, or Victoria and Rosie, or the Veng, or the girl who had reminded him so surprisingly of patches of colour. Tris took the bucket of water and filled the hen trough. The hens watched him from a distance, asking each other little questions. As Tris moved off around the house, he passed the old bath, clawed gryphon feet firmly grasping the earth, in the middle of a patch of self-seeding marigolds. Inside the house there was a tiny tiled cupboard which held a shower, the water for which was heated by solar power in the summer, and by the wood range in the winter. An indoor shower had been necessary so that they could get a permit for building the house. But for genuine washing, Tris's father usually ran a piece of hosepipe to the old bath outside. That way they had the fun of bathing by starlight, and it was easy to empty buckets of water over the garden afterwards. In the bath on summer nights, Randall would point out stars with wonderful names ('. . . there's Betelgeuse, and there's Alpha Centaurii. It's taken the light from that star four years to get here . . .'). When he thought of the bath, Tris loved his home and did not want to live anywhere else in the world. The pump, in a peaked house of its own, nestled up to the back of the house, but the lavatory was on its own as if it had some catching illness and had to be kept at a distance. And the noisy generator was even further away.

Bessie the goat did not seem particularly grateful for her water. She butted the dish, spilling most of it.

'All right! Don't, then!' Tris said. On his south side the brown flanks of the diving giant bristled unexpectedly with little green spikes – young pine trees which would one day be timber or wood pulp, depending on how they grew. Tris had helped his father plant them, and two hectares of pines were his and his alone. By the time he was properly grown up they would be grown up too, and he would be able to harvest them and sell the wood, and set himself up in business, and have a car of his own. He sat there dreaming of a Fiat X19, like the one Mr Partridge drove, or a yellow Lotus with a sun roof. Far below him the tide was out and a flock of white dots foraged on the bare mud and sand. Randall had once bought ten geese and a gander at an auction, but when he turned them loose to graze, they had run off to the edge of the sea and set up a hostile tribe of their own.

Tris sat down beside Bessie, rubbing her head between her horns. She tried to bunt him, but not particularly hard, just reminding him to give her the bread she knew he had brought with him. Tris fed her crusts, one by one, staring over at his pine trees and dreaming of the day when he and they would be grown tall. He wondered how he could want his home to stay the way it was for ever, and yet, at the same time want it different ... want it rich and powerful, with a sleek car and a garage and a tennis court, and an irrigation system shooting up a glittering spray that he could stand under on hot days.

'The windiest place in the whole damned world!' Tris's mother had once cried, and the insulted wind had lifted her red-rinsed hair, standing it on end and tangling it as she spoke. Tris remembered her striking at her own restless hair furiously, as if it were a swarm of stinging insects. 'My idea of paradise is a place where there's no wind.'

Now the wind beat in on Tris as he faced into it and he felt it trying to lift his hair in the same way it had lifted his mother's.

'Tris,' called Victoria, sounding like a sort-of mother. 'I've made you a drink with ice-cubes.'

If his own mother were to come back in the blue Triumph Herald, driving along the road, carefully avoiding the underrunners, and saw the 1969 Volkswagen 1500 parked there, looking so much at home, she might just drive silently away. No one would ever know she had called. All the same he liked Victoria, and the warm, amused smile that creased her face, and he also liked the thought of a drink with ice-cubes. Tris got to his feet and walked back to the house.

CHAPTER THREE

—— · ——

Scrambling to school the following morning Tris stopped where he had seen the girl look out at him. He studied the screen of leaves and listened for sneezes.

'Anyone there?' he asked, but there was no reply, so he coughed a bit, trying to pretend that he had only been coughing in the first place, stuck out his tongue at the morning, and walked on.

'Just having a go!' he muttered.

'*Have a go, and wind up wise!*' Selsey Firebone murmured. It was a motto from the planet Multitudino in the Dwango system.

Tris thought that when home-time came he would walk on the road instead of sliding along the Featherstonehaugh Children's Home fence. But later in the afternoon, as he came to the place where he usually left the road, he caught sight of a car – the Lotus again – crawling towards him like a slow, yellow missile, and he automatically jumped over the ditch and into the scrub. He and Selsey crept silently along the fence, saying nothing. There were his footprints in yesterday's loose dirt, but a new sprinkling of dirt had been flung across them. Tris did not turn his head, but his eyes shifted sideways, scanning the steel mesh fence and the leafy surface beyond it.

'Hey!' he said, almost to himself, trying to make it sound like the sort of thing one might say accidentally.

A flat, computerish voice answered from out of the leaves.

'Calling Selsey Firebone! Calling Selsey Firebone, the wonderful detective!'

Patches of rich transparent colour flashed into Tris's head. For a fraction of a second he understood it all, not only the splashes of colour but the place where he had once stood, enchanted by them. The memory flashed and flicked off before he could take control of it. The colours felt like part of an old story, something someone had read to him before he was able to read for himself.

'Are you hiding?' he asked cautiously.

There was a rustling on the Featherstonehaugh Children's Home side of the fence. The girl wriggled through the branches and leaves, pressing against the wire mesh like an animal in a zoo, staring at him with shining light-grey eyes. She hooked her fingers through the steel mesh and he saw she had coloured her badly-bitten fingernails with felt pens. Each nail was a different colour from the one next to it. She wore a bottle-green parka lined with salmon-pink, a black T-shirt with a high collar, and black trousers too short in the leg. Her feet, laced into running shoes, looked too big for her, while everything else looked too small.

'Hi!' she said, almost as if she expected him to be pleased to see her.

'Hi,' Tris replied. He heard himself sounding guarded and suspicious. Her expression grew suddenly guarded too.

'Do you live round here?' she asked.

'Down the road,' Tris answered, sounding puzzled as he pointed. 'I mean, *up* the road.'

She stared out at him between her hands. Tris felt like a prison visitor.

'They shoved me in here about a week ago,' she told him. 'I've been watching you going by every afternoon.'

She must have heard him talking to Selsey Firebone, but she didn't seem to be making fun of him, even secretly. Instead, she studied him intently, almost as if she were waiting for him to say some password that would allow her to come out from behind the wire.

'Your name's Tristram, isn't it?' she asked him.

'Tris!' Tris explained quickly.

'Tris!' she cried triumphantly, like someone finding the missing piece of a jigsaw puzzle. 'Short for Tristram! What does it mean?' she asked him next. Tris did not know.

'Tristram?' she repeated thoughtfully. 'Tristram!' She stared at him, saying his name as if she were tasting it before swallowing it. 'You ought to know what it *means* by now!'

'Names don't have to mean anything,' Tris replied defensively.

'I think they have to,' she said, 'I've got a book of names at home, not this Home, my other home. I look up what everyone's name means. That's how I find out what they're really like! My name's Winola and that means *friendly princess*.'

'Is it a Maori name?' Tris asked, though he didn't think it sounded Maori.

'The book says it's Teutonic,' Winola said doubtfully.

Tris thought it sounded like a brand of breakfast food. He could imagine Randall saying, 'Put milk on your Winola this morning.'

'I've gone to seven different schools in two years, seven counting this one, that is,' Winola went on. 'Seven's a mystic, magic number, so that means things are going to change for me pretty soon now. Where do you live?'

'Out on the point,' said Tris, pointing in the general direction of the invisible peninsula. 'The whole point belongs to us,' he added, boasting a little. But Winola thought he was beginning a Selsey Firebone game.

'Living on the point?' she repeated, as if she were getting the taste of the words. 'That's good! I live on the point, too,' she added, '. . . on the point of doom.' Then she looked up, grinned as if they were sharing a joke, edging back along the fence to the scraping and the freshly scattered earth.

'What are you digging? A grave for the Matron?' asked Tris, joking too. Winola was still smiling, but Tris immediately knew she was serious about her digging.

'I'm digging my way out!' she told him. 'I've got a spade hidden here. I stole it from their tool shed.' And indeed she did have a spade concealed among the dense leaves. 'It's taking me ages,' she said. 'The ground's hard, and I can only dig in free time. We don't get much free time,' she added. 'We mostly have dumb old school and organized play.'

'Is it free time now?' Tris asked.

'Yes,' said Winola. 'The other kids are playing down in the boys' forest, I think, but I peel off and get stuck in with the spade . . . the trusty spade,' she added, like someone trying to make a story more interesting by using powerful words. 'The outside kids think I'm reading inside, and the inside kids think I'm out in the forest.'

'What about the nurses?' asked Tris. 'Or the Matron?'

'Oh, all the staff are having afternoon tea and checking out their horoscopes in the paper,' Winola said cheerfully. 'They don't notice what's going on. Not for a bit, anyway.'

'Get out by the gate,' Tris suggested. 'I mean . . . there's a little gate that's always open.'

'But I don't want anyone else to know I've got a way out,' she said. 'It's got to be secret.'

'Why?' Tris asked, interested but puzzled.

Winola laughed. Her teeth were white and sharp — fox's teeth, thought Tris, though he'd never seen a fox in his life.

'There's someone after me. I have to have an escape route planned.'

'Who's after you?' Tris asked. But Winola's eyes suddenly lost their sharpness. Her whole face went vague. Her eyelids came down and half covered her astonishing light-grey eyes, almost as if she were suddenly on the point of going to sleep.

'Someone!' she said, even sounding drowsy. 'An evil villain, okay?'

'We should get someone on to him,' Tris remarked. 'Selsey Firebone,' he suggested daringly, surprising himself.

Her face grew sharp and foxy again.

'We need someone tough,' she said. 'Someone with a Lee Enfield 303 or a nuclear cannon. What about Selsey Firebone?'

'Selsey's really tough!' cried Tris quickly. 'He's got scars criss-crossed all over him.' As he spoke he found himself imagining something new about Selsey. 'He's had a lot of skin grafts so he's got black skin and brown skin and pink skin . . .'

'How come he's criss-crossed in scars if he's so tough?' Winola asked. 'I mean, how come anyone gets near enough to scar him?'

'Well, some of his enemies are tough too — tough and clever,' Tris began, suddenly eager to describe some Selsey adventure. Winola interrupted him.

30

'Fiendishly clever!' she exclaimed reprovingly, as if he had got some part of the story wrong. 'Say they're *fiendishly* clever!' Then she laughed. Tris paused and laughed too. By laughing they were somehow agreeing that this was a game, without actually having to say so.

'Probably they belong to B.I.C.,' Winola suggested, pressing her face against the wire.

'B.I.C.?' Tris asked. He didn't want a stranger adding anything into a private game, yet B.I.C. immediately sounded as if it had been part of the game from the beginning.

'Bureau of International Cruelty,' said Winola.

'Not "international"! "Intergalactic"!' Tris corrected her, growing even bolder as the idea seized him. 'The Bureau of Intergalactic Cruelty. The Veng belong to it.'

'The Veng? Do they have dagger claws?' asked Winola as if she couldn't quite remember something she had been told at school last week.

'They spit acid!' Tris explained.

'The one who's after me works for B.I.C.,' Winola said. 'He might even have Veng blood. If they *have* blood!'

'They have a sort of green porridge,' Tris said, surprising himself. He'd never thought of what kind of blood the Veng might have, and yet the answer leaped into his mouth as if it had been waiting. Winola smiled her moneybox smile. Her white pointed teeth were as startling in her brown face as her light-coloured eyes.

'I wish you had a spade, too,' she said. 'Then you could dig from your side.'

'Ours are all rusty,' said Tris, impressed by the sharp blade and the oiled wooden handle of the spade Winola held. The spades at home were blunt and the weathered handles could give you splinters. Randall and Tris both tended to leave tools outside after they had finished gardening. Leaning against the pump house at home were two spade heads with broken handles sticking out of them.

'I had to steal it from the tool shed,' Winola repeated in a matter-of-fact way. 'If I dig a little bit more I could push the spade under the fence to you and you could take a turn with the digging.'

But Tris did not feel like digging anything.

'I have to get home,' he said. 'I have to check up on my dad. There are two people who pretend to visit us, but they're trying to take over our organization.'

He was not quite inventing this time. That's what it sometimes felt like when Victoria came visiting. Winola simply nodded rather absent-mindedly. She struck the ground with the spade, which bounced back from the clay, ringing slightly, just as if she had driven it against iron.

'Will you be here tomorrow?' Tris asked.

'Probably,' Winola said. 'They're looking for a foster home for me but I bet they don't find one.'

Tris began to move away. Then he paused.

'Won't the Matron protect you from the villain who's after you?' he asked.

'I don't know,' Winola said. 'She might. But the thing is that people trust him. He *sounds* as if you should trust him. He's . . .' She screwed up her face. 'You know . . . sincere! Charming!'

'*He'll have his work cut out if he takes us on,*' Selsey Firebone said in his lazy, clenched-teeth voice. Tris was startled to hear Selsey's voice speaking not to him but, for the first time he could remember, to someone else. If Winola had looked scornful or acted as if the voice were nothing but a joke, perhaps Selsey would not have spoken again. But she nodded in the same absent-minded way, staring rather gloomily at the clay.

'Right!' she said in a clenched-teeth voice of her own. 'He's bitten off more than he can chew.' It was as if Selsey Firebone's twin sister had spoken back to him. More than that, it sounded to Tris like Winola's own secret voice . . . the voice that went best with her sharp white teeth and her close-cut hair.

Tris backed away, half wanting to stay and to hear her talk again. But she was chopping at the hard ground with the Featherstonehaugh Children's Home spade.

'See you, then,' he said, a little disappointed because she didn't seem to care that he was going.

'Right!' she said and chopped again. Tris saw a few crumbs of clay break free at the edge of her hole. Then she looked up.

'Charming means *magical*,' she told him. 'I just worked it out. If you charm someone you put a spell on them. My enemy could charm the Matron, and she'd try to make me talk to him.' Tris nodded, but said nothing. He believed Winola was inventing her villain as details occurred to her, just as he himself had suddenly added patches of different coloured skin on to Selsey Firebone.

Walking along the fence away from her, Tris imagined the thud of the spade was beating an underground message in code all the way up the hill through the grass tunnel, right to his own gate.

CHAPTER FOUR

___ . ___

Walking home, Tris swung his schoolbag backwards and forwards until he felt that the bag was somehow swinging itself, and he was just an odd thinking part of it.

After a while he turned and glanced back the way he had come. Featherstonehaugh Children's Home nestled back among its trees. The house was barely visible, but he could see distant children running across an uneven triangle of lawn, a wedge of light-green driven between the darker trees. Winola would not be one of them. She would be crammed between the shrubbery and the high steel fence, striking the ground with her spade, trying to dig her way out. The game they had played still seemed to be going on around him. Tris did not want to go back to everyday life just yet.

The track ran between the tussocks like a parting in the hair of the land. Sun-dried grasses rustled around him, but there was no sound of cars or spades up here. He had entered a zone of silence.

'No more messages,' he said aloud, imagining that members of B.I.C. were constantly tapping out vibration messages to the Veng, and that he and Selsey had to decipher them.

'*Up we go!*' said Selsey Firebone. '*Don't worry! We'll break the code later.*'

Abruptly the ground gaped, opening a mouth hairy with grass. But Tris knew this hole well and lowered himself into it. Although he was aware that holes like this could collapse unexpectedly on whoever was in them, once he was underground he felt surprisingly secure. It was funny to think that something as menacing as an underrunner could be a safe hiding-place as well. The innocent, kindly smell of earth and dried grass surrounded him. A hole like this was much too dry for the Veng, who liked to enfold themselves in slime.

Tris had always liked the part in *The Wind in the Willows* when Rat and Mole, visiting Mole's old home, found at the end of a tunnel smelling of earth, a tidy forecourt with statues and ferns, a skittle alley and a large silver ball that reflected everything all wrong. It seemed as if it should be possible, supposing he worked hard enough, that he too could make such a forecourt in the opening of one of the underrunners. Though Tris knew it could never really be done, the idea played on the edge of his mind, tossed between possibility and impossibility.

After a moment, he lifted up some clods of dried grass and checked his shoebox of supplies. He was tempted to eat the peanuts, but knew it might mean the difference between life and death. If you eat your supplies, you have to come out of your hole and look for more. Tris imagined bringing his father here during a time of military crisis. They would sit and eat peanuts until the enemy air attack, or offshore bombardment, or whatever it was that was raging on the surface, went away. 'Thank God one of us had a bit of common sense and foresight,' Randall would say gratefully.

'*Those peanuts will be there when we need them,*' said Selsey Firebone. At that moment, compared with Selsey Firebone, Victoria and Rosie, Sylvia Collins and the Morley boys, even his father out on the point, were faint and insubstantial.

Tris sank into his story with relief. He and Selsey were hiding out in the cave system of Kruj, the third planet of the Dwango system, hunted by the blind cave dwellers who moved with such shocking agility.

'*The Moleymen!*' said Selsey. Tris hesitated. In *The Wind in the Willows* Mole was a gentle animal. '*The Mewlymen,*' Selsey Firebone quickly corrected himself. '*They make a mewing sound as they move.*'

'With shocking agility,' Tris added aloud, determined to keep those words in his story. A moment later he found himself wondering if Winola were still digging away in the shrubbery, for he believed he could feel the rhythm of her spade, faint but determined, travelling along wormholes in space, science fiction underrunners too small to be seen by the human eye, coming up through the palms of his hands as they rested against the walls of the hole.

'*We must rescue her,*' Selsey said.

'She's rescuing herself,' Tris replied and Selsey fell silent.

The vibration of the spade seemed so distinct that Tris scrambled out of the hole to look around. But there was no one in sight, only an empty Coke tin left behind, he supposed, by some casual wanderer. If only they had known that there were four tins of Coke and some peanuts hidden under a clod at the back of the underrunner! Though he listened hard, Tris could not hear anything but larks and the hum of a distant car.

It was only when he had climbed to the top of the last hill that the sound of the spade on the iron clay came back again, but not because he was being haunted, or spied on by B.I.C., or because the sound of Winola's digging was following him. Below him lay his house, his home, the cat flag waving over it, lapped by its curious jumble of machinery, tumbledown hen houses, the old bath, motorbikes that did not go, and so on. Randall was outside. He was digging steadily. Victoria stood beside him, holding up a long rod, rather like a lance. Rosie crouched between them, staring down into the hole, rather as the small cat, Puzzle, sometimes stared into a rat hole waiting for prey to come out. From up here they looked like a pioneer family in an old picture, while Tris, who should have been there in the centre of it all, was outside the picture frame, looking in.

He began to run downhill, becoming an aircraft, a

little Cessna, with Selsey Firebone at the controls, swooping down in a long, low, lazy glide, effortless and happy, frightening everyone as he zoomed over them. Selsey would pull the stick back and he would swoop up again, looping the loop, turning over and over in the autumn air. Tris's thoughts flew, but his feet never quite left the ground. He came running down, scattering cats and hens. His last leap felt like a particularly high one, for the slope fell away sharply beneath him. As he left the ground he saw water leap too, leap from where his father was digging. He's found a spring, thought Tris for a second, at the height of his own leap. Our water troubles are over. But as he came down to earth a strong smell, a dirty smell, the foul smell of old soapy water suddenly disturbed after sulking for days, rushed up to meet him.

'Ratty!' shouted Rosie triumphantly.

'Tris?' said Randall, looking up startled, as if Tris were the last person he had expected to see falling out of the air. Tris thudded down, his knees buckling, staggering left, correcting course, staggering right, coming to rest an inch from Randall's elbow.

'I've had to clear that drain,' Randall explained. 'Water started to come back up through the plug hole of the shower.'

'And I'm just helping,' said Victoria, looking guilty.

Nobody would help with a blocked drain out of mere friendship, Tris thought. She really is out to get him. Aloud, he said. 'Pooooh! It *stinks*!'

'Old soapy water from the washing,' Randall said ruefully. 'You can see what's happened, though. Loose soil's worked its way in between the field pipes and blocked the system.'

Rosie ran at Tris, making roaring noises, threatening him with one of his own plastic dinosaurs . . . a stegosaurus. Tris pretended to collapse on to the grass, feeling his glasses seesaw across the bridge of his nose. Rosie shrieked with triumph and excitement.

'Oh, oh Rosie!' sang Victoria, making it sound like the first line of a song. 'Leave the poor man alone. He's had a hard day. Don't put up with it, Tris!'

Rosie's shrieking was remarkable, either for a child or a stegosaurus. She dinosaured Tris fiercely, until Victoria came up behind and put some sort of motherly hammerlock on her.

'You don't have to. *I* don't mind!' Tris said.

'She only does it because she likes you,' Victoria explained.

'I wish I was half as tough,' Tris said, putting his glasses straight again.

'Watch her and pick up some hints,' said his father.

'It wouldn't work,' said Tris. 'You've got to be born like that.'

'What do you think you were born like?' asked Victoria.

'An owl,' said his father before Tris could answer.

'Just because of my glasses,' Tris said. But he didn't mind the thought of being an owl and flying silently by night, a little light bony body, plumed up and softened with feathers. 'Are there any Anzac biscuits left?'

'A few,' said Randall. 'And what have you been up to today?'

'Nothing,' Tris said.

'You must have done *something*,' Randall persisted, taking the long rod from Victoria and trying to bend it round some sort of corner in the drain.

'Yes, but it was *like* nothing. I don't want to *talk* about it,' Tris said. 'I'm going up to the house.'

'My day was like nothing, too,' Randall agreed, 'until I began to smell the drain, and *that* was like nothing on earth!'

'*Nothing on earth! A Veng acid attack!*' said Selsey Firebone, speaking inside Tris, not outside in world space. Tris imagined Selsey moving through invisible tunnels in his brain. Winola, Selsey, B.I.C. had not vanished. They were all there, waiting for drains and Anzac biscuits and Rosie and Victoria to go out like the tide. Then Tris's mind would turn a flip and the world would turn over with it. Out would come Selsey and Winola to inhabit this other place, the same but different, rather like that other reflected world the tide left behind.

'I'll come with you,' Victoria said.

As they walked past Bessie, the goat gave a bleat that sounded as if she were laughing.

Tris scrambled up towards the house, followed by Victoria, who climbed slowly, carrying Rosie on her hip to get her safely over a thistly bit. As she climbed, Victoria sang. She had a voice with a life of its own, for it never stuck to a tune but swooped around it – up, over, in and out – coming back to the tune it had deserted only to desert it again, to do something unexpected up in the high notes. She didn't just *sing* songs ... she played with them, like the cats played with leaves in autumn. Sometimes Rosie joined in, but she always sang words ... usually the name of some food or other. 'Ice cream! Ice cream!' she would sing. Or 'Fish and chi-i-i-ps!'

As they walked past the bath in the garden Victoria caught up with him. 'Sorry to be here yet again, Mr Ratty,' said Victoria. 'I'm between jobs and I do like visiting your house.'

'Rosie's been playing with my dinosaurs again,' Tris said. 'She's stolen my stegosaurus.'

'I'm sorry,' Victoria said. 'She climbs on chairs, and I don't always notice.'

She sounded so apologetic that Tris knew he couldn't complain any more.

'Do any of the kids from school visit you here?' Victoria asked him. 'It seems a wonderful place for playing and just running around.'

Tris thought of his father's ponytail, the outside lavatory, the bath in the marigolds and the usual after-school lack of cake.

'I don't want visitors,' he said, trying to sound light-hearted. 'I mean, visitors come here sometimes, but the best part is when they go away.'

CHAPTER FIVE

The following day was Thursday.

'Soon be Saturday,' Guy Morley shouted, zig-zagging backwards and forwards across the road on his ten-speed. He and Brian were going with their father and an uncle on a motor rally on Saturday. They were driving a modified Nissan. 'I'm navigating!' Guy boasted. 'Me, too!' echoed Brian.

Sylvia was going to spend a weekend with her grandmother so that her parents could go away together. She talked about this as they went past the yellow and black A.A. sign, *Featherstonehaugh Children's Home*.

'Fan-shaw, Fan-shaw, Fan-shaw!' Tris sang softly to himself, listening to the story of Sylvia's parents and their rocky marriage.

'Granny says having children took the romance out of their marriage,' Sylvia told him.

'Yes, but some people get sick of romance,' Tris replied.

Sylvia shrugged.

'I don't know,' she said. 'See you tomorrow!' Then she disappeared up her drive. Tris walked on, uphill, downhill, looked both ways, and dived into the road-side scrub on to his private path.

Winola was in plain view today, fingers hooked through the mesh, waiting for him to appear.

When she saw him coming she threw herself on the ground. At first Tris thought she was pretending that she had been wounded by the Veng. Then he saw that she was actually wriggling under the fence. The hollow was deep enough for her to squeeze through. She got to her feet on his side of the fence, scraped and smeared, but smiling as he came up to her.

'Pretty radical, eh?' she said.

Tris was impressed.

'I didn't really think you would,' he said. 'Dig it out, I mean!'

'*Get stuck in mate, and you can move the world,*' said Selsey Firebone.

'Well, I did move a bit of it,' Winola agreed. 'If the enemy comes asking for me I'll just say, "Hang on while I go to the bog." Then I'll duck into the girls' bathroom and out the window! Then into the trees and under the fence and off. Now, show me some good hiding places.'

'We'll have to go right past the gate,' Tris said.

'You go first,' Winola suggested. 'Check it out, and then beckon to me. Is there anywhere to hide on the other side of the gate?'

'Not until the corner,' Tris said. 'There's a good place to hide about a hundred metres off.' A hundred metres was a Selsey Firebone guess. Perhaps Winola knew this.

'I just want to know what direction to take when I'm escaping,' she explained, giving him a look which Tris felt was mainly intended for Selsey Firebone. They came out of the scrub and hesitated.

'Ready?' asked Tris.

'I'm making myself thin!' Winola replied.

'Why?' Tris said. 'You're already the skinniest person I've ever seen.'

'Just as well, or I'd have had to dig out twice as much from under the fence,' she said. 'It's a real help to be skinny. For hiding and squeezing, anyway!' Tris imagined that, if Winola drew herself in and stood sideways, the Veng would see nothing but a puckered line wavering in the air.

He ran under the big notice that said *Featherstonehaugh Children's Home* and stared in at the gate. He could hear the shouts of children playing, could see a young woman crossing the lawn, holding hands with a tiny child barely able to walk.

'Come on!' he called.

Winola followed him past the gate.

'How can Feather-stone-haugh ever, ever possibly turn into Fanshaw?' he asked her, thinking she might know, being a Children's Home child.

'It just does!' she told him. 'It doesn't have to make sense.'

She spoke as if sense were a luxury – like a tennis court – which Tris shouldn't even begin to think about.

'I reckon it's a sign!' she added, as they moved up the road, leaving the gate behind them.

'I know it's a sign,' Tris said. 'The A.A. put them up for motorists.'

'Not just a road sign!' Winola answered impatiently. 'A sign of life ... just to warn you it doesn't mean what it looks like. Where do we go now?'

'Into the ditch,' Tris instructed her. 'It's dry at this time of the year so we can crawl right along it.'

'Hey! Great!' Winola cried softly. She was thrilled with the tunnel, and the flicker of sky between the brown interlocking stems overhead. There was a faint grassy rasping as they scuffled past.

'*Can't be too careful!*' said Selsey Firebone.

Winola grinned. Tris thought, once again, her foxy grin was more for Selsey Firebone than it was for him.

'This tunnel's a fire risk in summer,' he told her sternly.

'Well, I won't worry about it until it actually *is* on fire,' Winola replied.

As they reached a place in the ditch where the sides widened, they heard the sound of a car going past on the road above them. It sounded so close that the gravel seemed to be crunching right in their ears. Winola flattened herself on to the floor of the ditch. Tris, impressed by her alarm, copied her. No wonder she had wormed her way into his game when she believed so strongly in her own. His heart banged in his chest as if there really were something frightening – some Veng or yellow-rocket-android – speeding by on the road up there. The car roared uphill, unaware of their presence. Tris and Winola sat and listened as it cornered above them. Dust sifted down on them through the loose weave of the grass. Winola's face was crossed with shadows. She looked as if she were being scribbled out.

'What's it like in the Home?' Tris asked her.

'It's okay,' said Winola. 'The food's pretty good. I mean it's not that healthy, but everyone likes it.'

'They're supposed to give you healthy stuff,' Tris said disapprovingly.

'Yeah!' Winola agreed enthusiastically. 'Everything we eat should be raw. Cooking kills all food spirits.'

This was not quite what Tris had meant by being healthy.

'Everyone cooks!' he protested. 'Cave men discovered fire and started civilization going.'

'Food is full of spirits,' Winola persisted. 'You should eat it raw. Then the spirits flow into your spirit and you get all charged up with nature. Cooking kills the spirits, and the food you eat is dead.'

'Well, I don't want to eat anything alive!' Tris replied.

Winola was silent, thinking this over.

'Not alive like you or me,' she said at last. 'Grated carrot doesn't *feel* anything! Anyhow, nearly everything at the Home is cooked.'

'Do you eat it?' asked Tris.

'Of course,' said Winola. 'I have to or I'd starve. But I know what I'm eating . . . dead food!'

'Do you have anyone else in your room with you?' Tris asked, wondering how Winola got on with other girls.

'There are seventeen girls in the girls' dormitory at present,' Winola told him. 'That's a lot. I'm thirteen and just about the oldest. I'm almost too old to be in this Home, but they didn't know where to put me, and I've been here twice before. There are five kids too little to go to school, and there's one kid who's a bed-wetter. We're not allowed to make fun of her, in case it makes her worse. But other kids do . . . you know, in free time, when no one's listening, they whisper, "Are you going to wet your bed again tonight, Jolene?" and then they hold their noses and all that. But I don't make fun of her,' she added. 'I can't be bothered.'

'Why are you there?' asked Tris. Almost at once he thought it might be a tactless question, but Winola didn't seem to mind.

'I'm not a bed-wetter,' she said. 'Every now and then my mother tries to kill herself. Last year, and again this year. She's okay most of the time, but every now and then she goes . . . you know . . . crazy!'

Tris felt obliged to show that Winola was not the only one that terrible things could happen to.

'My mother ran away,' he said. 'She and my dad used to fight a lot, and then she took our car. It was

49

a Triumph Herald.' But at least his mother was alive and free somewhere. She might turn up at any moment, her bracelets and silver chains jingling, floating in a cloud of flowery scent.

'Cars!' Winola said. 'We've had nothing but cars. Once we lived in a house that had seven broken cars around it, and bits of other cars as well.'

'Didn't any of them go?' asked Tris.

'Some of them did sometimes,' said Winola. 'Have you ever heard of an elephants' graveyard?'

Tris thought for a moment. 'In Africa!' he said at last. 'When elephants know they're going to die, they find their way there.'

'Our house was a graveyard for cars,' Winola said. 'Dying cars came secretly through the streets.' She made, with astonishing accuracy, the sound of a stumbling car engine. 'And then they fell to bits on our lawn.'

It was when he saw her sly, dry grin as she said this that Tris suddenly knew he really liked her.

'I used to read the funeral service over them,' Winola went on.

'Did they rest in peace?' Tris asked.

'They rested in pieces,' Winola said, still grinning. 'Ted, the boyfriend my mother had then, was a car vampire. He called himself a mechanic but he really was a car vampire, sinking his screwdriver fangs into old cars, draining out their oil. Heh! Heh! Heh!' Winola gave a vampire-ish laugh, then asked, 'Do you live with your father now?'

'Yes,' Tris said. 'He's a sort of artist. He does drawings for landscape gardeners.' It sounded a pale thing for a father to be when you were talking to someone whose mother's boyfriend had been a car vampire. 'Do you still live in the car graveyard?'

'No,' said Winola. 'Ted met up with someone he liked better than my mother, and we moved back to our old house. Do you ever see your mother?'

'No!' said Tris. He had never found it so easy to say before. 'She took off to Australia. Dad says she'll come back one day. He says she'll want to find out how I'm getting on. He says she's so mad at him and the way things turned out for them that she wants to forget everything to do with him. But he says it's not my fault.'

'Hey,' said Winola, smiling as if this was a joke they could share. 'They always say it's not your fault. Mind you, I already know it's not my fault. Big deal, eh!'

'Big deal!' Tris repeated, copying her scornful tone.

'Social workers always tell you that it's not your fault, like they were giving you really great news that you didn't know already. Big deal! You're still stuck with it,' Winola said. 'But I'm tough.'

They scrambled out of the ditch on the top of the hill and stood under a gum tree looking out over the bay and the barren, sun-drenched hills that surrounded it. From here, there was not one roof to be seen. It was as if they were the only people in an early version of the world.

'So where do you live?' asked Winola.

'Out there!' said Tris, pointing. From this angle the diving man looked pleated, as if someone had tried to cram him back flat against the mainland. In the gullies the bush was so dark a green as to be almost black. Tris's house was invisible, but Winola reacted as if it were right in front of them.

'You live in *that* house!' she cried. Her whole face was bright with interest. 'The up-in-the-air one on sticks?'

'On poles!' Tris explained. 'It's meant to be like that.'

'I can see that house from the girls' dormitory window. I thought it was the last house in the world. I didn't know anyone *lived* there.' Winola stopped and suddenly gasped. Then she pulled a man's handkerchief out of her ski jacket pocket and sneezed.

'Why?' asked Tris. 'I mean, why the *last* house?'

'Because it looks like the world has been devastated by nuclear attacks.' Her voice grew solemn and hollow. 'Everything is dead but one person, and that person is the last person in the world, living on the edge of the sea. You lucky pig.' She peered at the pleats in the land as if she might be able to look right through them if she tried hard enough. Then she sneezed again.

'You're always sneezing,' Tris said. 'Have you got a cold?'

'Hay fever,' Winola explained. 'It's because we've been under this grass. Every spring I have to take antihistamine to stop sneezing. What's it like . . . living out there?'

'It's like living in a desert,' said Tris. 'We haven't got enough water. Most of what we plant dies.' He heard his voice sounding gloomy yet proud at the same time.

'It's just terrific, though,' said Winola. 'If it was me, I'd love to be the last person in the world living there. You could guard that narrow bit, and no one could come and get at you! You'd be safe.'

'*Helicopters!*' exclaimed Selsey Firebone.

'Oh, yeah! I suppose,' said Winola slowly. 'Get a Lee Enfield! No, an AK47.'

Tris didn't like to tell her that he didn't know what an AK47 was.

'*Make it hard for them,*' said Selsey Firebone, but he didn't know either.

'We could hide in the tunnels,' said Tris. 'Come and see!' Suddenly he was longing to show her the underrunners and his store of baked beans and the tin-opener.

Winola turned and looked at him seriously.

'Real tunnels?'

'*Underrunners!*' said Selsey Firebone.

'No, but really *truly*!' she repeated.

'*Yes!*' cried Tris, affronted because she seemed so doubtful. 'Come on! I'll show you.'

She might know what an AK47 was, but *he* knew all about underrunners.

'I can't,' said Winola. 'I'm not quite ready yet.

Not organized! I'll have to get back or they'll look for me.' She dropped back into the ditch, leaving Tris standing there, already feeling a little lonely. It had been fun having Winola beside him, scrambling up the grassy tunnel right to his gate.

'Well,' he said a little blankly to the air over the tunnel. 'See you tomorrow.' The grass blades had folded over her. She was nothing but pieces of colour and one clearly-seen grey eye looking up at him.

'See you tomorrow!' she answered.

'See you tomorrow, mate!' said Selsey Firebone, and Tris heard Winola laugh a little. He caught the gleam of her pointed teeth behind the criss-cross screen of the long grass before she crept away. Tris watched her go, and some time after she had vanished, when there was nothing to show that there was a live girl creeping down the hidden ditch, he suddenly heard her sneeze.

'One sneeze like that, and the Veng would be after her,' said Selsey Firebone. Tris nodded, and the blunt faceless head of his shadow walking beside him nodded, too.

CHAPTER SIX

——— · ———

Tris checked the letter-box: no letter from Sydney. No letters at all! He set off home with a bouncing step. The graded road bent a little, responding to the curve of the land. As Tris followed the curve too, he came upon a stranger standing on the road in front of him, looking straight back at him through a pair of binoculars. The binoculars were black, the man's hair was bleached a yellowish white.

People often walked along the peninsula, particularly at weekends, drawn by the way it stretched itself out towards the head of the bay. Sometimes Tris, hiding in the mouth of an underrunner, or wriggling through the grass and tussock, practised his tracking and spying skills on them. He would hear them exclaiming over the little beaches that fringed its corrugated sides, or the trembling reflections of the hills. But such hikers and accidental wanderers always looked out to the head of the bay. This man had his back to the beautiful view.

Tris paused. To sidle past a stranger, even a friendly one, would break the flow of secrets running through him, so he turned, planning to swarm quietly up the bank and take some other track home. But it was too late. The man was already lowering the binoculars and smiling at him. Now that his face was not covered by the binoculars, Tris could see the man's bright eyes and tanned face. He wore a denim jacket, blue jeans, and a black jersey with a high-rolled collar. But in spite of his cold-weather clothes he looked as if he had just spent a week in the sun on the Gold Coast. He gave Tris a warm, quick smile.

'Good afternoon!' he said.

'Hi!' said Tris, coming closer. There was no sense in hiding now that he had been seen.

'Great day, Monsieur,' said the man. He looked over his shoulder towards the end of the peninsula. 'Off for a bit of a ramble?'

'Sort of,' Tris said politely. 'Well, I live here.'

The man stared around him as if the idea of anyone living there among the tussocks surprised him.

'What? Out here? In some rabbit hole?'

'On the point!' said Tris, pointing. 'My dad built our house himself.'

In those days there had been enough money to hire a truck. He could remember Randall and his builder-friend, Noel, wrestling planks and boards and second-hand doors down the last few yards of the slope.

'Wonderful place to live,' the man said politely. He had a soft, husky voice that reminded Tris of a friend of his father's who lectured at the university in the city over the hill and who talked about words and the meaning of words ... a man who would look at a word like *Featherstonehaugh* and know immediately why it was pronounced Fanshaw. This man sounded as if he had the same sort of knowledge. However, what he actually said was, 'Would you care to crack open a Coke, Monsieur?'

'What?' asked Tris.

'I bought a couple of cans at the shop back by the school, but one's been more than enough for me, and I can't be bothered carting it all the way back to the car,' the man said, pointing out a big binocular case, its strap trailing through the grass like a thin black snake. It was open and Tris could see it held one unopened can of Coke. An empty can and a half-empty whisky bottle stood beside it in the grass.

Tris sat down on the edge of the track. To right and left of him, dry summer thistles, goblins with many spiky heads, scratched at the softly moving air.

'Empty, though, isn't it?' the man said uneasily. 'People always think New Zealand's green, green, nothing but bloody green. They forget the bits like this. Right on the coast, too!'

'We don't get much rain in summer,' said Tris.

'That's okay. I hate green anyway,' the man replied. 'To hell with green. Concrete the whole country, and paint it black. Spirit's Bay down to Stewart Island ... that's what I say!' He looked at Tris and gave a smile so gentle that it changed his harsh words to some sort of joke. 'I'll bet they don't teach you that at school!'

'No,' said Tris. 'We have conservation and saving the ozone layer.'

'I'll just bet you do,' the man said. 'Schools are supposed to prepare you for life, but I'll tell you this for free, Boss. They *hide* it, that's what I reckon. The powers-that-be don't want to know themselves, and they don't want anyone else to find out, either.'

'I know already, though,' Tris said, believing he did.

'It'd kill me, living out here,' the man said, just as if that was what they had been talking about. 'I need light, beautiful women, and music, music, music! What about you, Monsieur?'

'I like it,' Tris answered.

'You'd need to,' the man said. 'How does your lady mother manage, stuck out on the end of this rock?'

'She hated it,' said Tris, astonished to find himself telling this old story for the second time in about ten minutes. 'She ran away and took the car.'

'Women!' said the man. 'Can't get along with them, can't get along without them, can we?' He still spoke as if Tris were a man of his own age. 'Was she pretty, your mum?'

'Yes,' Tris said, and once again the picture came into his mind of a pretty woman with long black hair, silver chains around her neck, and a bracelet heavy with charms dangling from her wrist. He even remembered one of the charms, a little windmill with sails that really went round. He remembered being allowed to turn the sails, and breathing in the flowery scent of his mother as he did so. He remembered her rare, awkward hugs. But, as the picture of the black-haired woman with silver chains formed in his mind, he knew he had got it all wrong. The chains and the bracelet were right, but his mother had had brown hair with a red rinse in it. What he was remembering was the hair of Dearie Tyrone, the mother of Tod, Damon and Cissy.

Quickly, he adjusted the memory, giving the faceless woman red-rinsed hair, but he was no longer sure he really was recalling his true mother. He tried to put her out of his mind.

'The pretty ones are the worst, by God!' the man was saying. He sighed. 'Well, no clues there. Back to civilization.' He was just about to fit his binoculars back into the case, when he paused and held them out to Tris.

'Have a go, Monsieur!' he suggested.

Tris took them, partly out of politeness. Randall's binoculars sat on the chest of drawers beside the dinosaur collection, and Tris had often studied the hills, the horizon and even passing ships with them. All the same, it seemed rude not to encourage friendliness. The hilltops wavered in and out of sight as Tris tipped his head back. These binoculars were too big ... older and heavier and harder to hold still than the ones he was used to. Besides, though binoculars let you look closely at certain things, they only showed little disconnected details. To know what the hilltops were really like you had to see the sky above and the water below. And then he suddenly remembered the man had not been looking at the hilltops. He had been pointing in quite a different direction. On an impulse, Tris lifted the binoculars once more, swinging them to look behind him. For a moment he couldn't quite make out what he was seeing. A patch of lighter green . . . children running and playing. Flowers. Fairyland. He took the binoculars away and blinked. The green became a distant lopsided wedge, the children shrank to coloured beetles, zig-zagging across it.

Of course, he was looking back into the Featherstonehaugh Children's Home, and seeing the piece of lawn that showed between its trees. That was what the man had been looking at.

'I've got my rights, you know,' the man said suddenly. He was talking to himself. In a way he had been talking to himself all the time, bouncing a few words off Tris without really thinking about who he was talking to. Now, he slipped the binoculars into their case, bending forward as he did so. His cheeks seemed to fall forward just a little from the bones of his face; his skin seemed to wrinkle under its tan. He was not as young as he had looked from a distance. His bleached hair did not quite match the rest of him. Tris noticed how the backs of his fingers gleamed for he wore several rings . . . a gold wedding ring, and another gold ring on his little finger, as well as a silver ring with a dragon's face on his right hand. Having hung the binoculars round his neck he slipped sun-glasses from his pocket. Just before he put them on Tris looked up into his vivid, smiling, blue eyes, and felt as if he were looking past the smile and into a curious blankness. There was no one at home behind the smiling surface. And only when the man had put on the dark glasses did Tris recognize, for the first time, the driver of the yellow Lotus who had asked the way to the Featherstonehaugh Children's Home the day before yesterday. His grey hair was now blond, but it was the same man all right, though his car was nowhere in sight.

'See you around, Monsieur!' the man said cheerfully, and began walking back towards the road. Tris watched him, but the stranger did not turn once, marching straight to the gate, climbing it, turning to the left and vanishing. He had taken his whisky, but had left the two Coke cans sitting in the grass. Littering, Tris thought indignantly, although he had emptied one of the cans himself. Just what you'd expect of a man who hates green. He put the Coke cans into his schoolbag and continued on his way home.

As he picked through the debris that surrounded his house, he saw Randall looking through the double doors and then hurriedly pulling the curtains across them. Victoria's there, Tris thought, looking suspiciously around for her car. But when he pushed in between the curtains and into the big room he found his father quite alone, standing in a space filled with rainbows. Tris stood, fixed with amazement, staring at the ceiling which was suddenly painted with short bars of bright, clear colours. Randall had hung glass prisms on various lengths of cotton from the top of the little sunny nor-west window.

'What do you think?' he asked Tris anxiously. 'Have some refreshments and enjoy the rainbows!'

A jug of apple juice and two Anzac biscuits were set out on the ironing board which doubled as a coffee table.

'Thanks!' Tris said in astonishment. 'What are we doing this for?'

'Why not?' asked Randall.

'Yes, but why?' asked Tris. He couldn't understand it. 'Have you finished your work early?'

'No,' said Randall, 'but I just thought it couldn't be much fun for you, coming home after a hard day at school, and either finding me unblocking drains, or locked away like some sort of mad monk in a monastery.'

Tris sat down slowly.

'Go on!' cried Randall. 'Encourage me! Then I'll ask you about your day and tell you about mine.'

'It's a bit like getting home and finding I'm a sort of visitor,' said Tris. He saw Tab and Puzzle sitting patiently by the stove, tricked into thinking that dinnertime was closer than it really was. 'Did you do this when I was little? Make rainbows?'

'No!' said Randall. 'This is one-off job. A new idea.'

'I remember it, though,' Tris said. 'I've seen it before . . . these colours. Not here, but somewhere!'

'I thought about it the other day,' Randall explained. 'You come home. I shout out to you to make me coffee and ask you what's happened in your day, and you say "Nothing!". And that's it. That's our after-school life. I ought to take a break when you come home and talk to you more.'

'You don't have to,' said Tris, embarrassed. A sudden thought struck him. 'Did Victoria tell you to talk to me?'

'No,' said Randall. 'Not quite. Well, we did mention it in passing. She's not too sure whether you like her or not.'

'I do like her,' Tris cried. 'I mean she's okay, but the kids at school say she's going to catch you.'

Randall leaped to his feet again.

'I'm not some sort of *fish*,' he cried indignantly. Then his indignation died away. 'Anyway, would you mind if she did catch me?' he asked inquisitively.

Tris shrugged and mumbled. He had had a general-knowledge test at school earlier in the day, and now he suddenly felt that he was going through another one.

'Come on! What *would* you think?' Randall asked.

'I don't know,' Tris cried. 'Well . . .' he began and then stopped.

'Well, what?'

'Suppose my mother came back and . . .' Tris stopped again. 'I mean I know she *won't*, but suppose she *did*. Sylvia's mother came back.'

Randall sat down again. His thin face had looked both anxious and eager. This was something he had thought about so often that answers came out of him quite easily.

'She won't,' he said. 'At least, she'll come back to see *you*, some day, but she won't stay. She didn't *like* being married to me – not really – though she tried to like it for a while. And . . . don't get this wrong, Tris . . . she really loved you, as a baby, as a boy, but somehow she didn't enjoy being a mother! She tried hard, but it never worked out. However, don't you worry too much about that, it's not your fault!'

Winola's face, striped like a tiger's with the shadows of grass, sprang back into Tris's mind. He saw her sharp white teeth. 'Big deal!' she had said.

'Big deal!' said Tris, tilting his head back and looking at his father round a smear on his glasses. Randall's blue eyes widened slightly, growing more wary.

'I just thought I'd remind you,' Randall answered. 'It's a long time since we've talked about it, and you're getting older so quickly. The thing is, some day she will come back and tell you all this herself, but she won't ever come home to stay.'

'You don't have to counsel me,' Tris said, for suddenly it seemed that the rainbows and the apple juice were nothing but a sort of counselling aimed at getting him to like Victoria. 'I said Victoria was okay, so no more counselling.'

'We're talking,' his father said, looking hurt. 'That's all counselling is, talking things over, working things out.'

'Yes, but sometimes you begin to talk in a special counselling voice,' Tris said. 'All quiet and wise and understanding. I don't want to come home from school and get counselled. I haven't done anything.'

Randall looked as if he might laugh, but it was hard to make out just what he might be laughing at.

'I don't even remember her that well,' Tris went on. 'Mum, I mean. Actually, someone asked about her today, and when I remembered her, she was sort of mixed up with Dearie from next door.'

Randall frowned as if he, too, were struggling to remember back over the years.

'Dearie Tyrone,' he said at last. 'God, yes! Poor old Dearie!'

'What was poor about her?' asked Tris, glad to stop talking about his mother.

'Well, she was one of the most beautiful women I've ever known,' his father said, 'and that's supposed to be an advantage. But it was like a doom for Dearie. Do you remember her kids at all?'

'I remember Cissy,' Tris said. 'She had long hair with tangles. I remember Tod reckoned his name meant 'death' in German, so Cecily and I used to call Tod and Damon – Death and Demon. There was Dearie, Death and Demon in that family.'

'That sounds about right!' said Randall.

'I remembered Dearie's hair, but Mum's charm bracelet,' said Tris. 'She used to let me turn the little windmill round.' He saw Randall was about to speak, and added hastily, 'No conselling!'

'I'm just trying to be fatherly,' said Randall.

'You don't have to,' said Tris. 'You're fatherly enough already.'

CHAPTER SEVEN

——— · ———

Tris woke up with a cat asleep on top of him. He knew at once from its feeling of fatness that it was Tab nestling close to him, enjoying his spare warmth. Outside, he could hear bellbirds, which came out of the bush every autumn looking for nectar in the throats of people's garden flowers.

Randall's footsteps sounded quick and lively as if he had been up for some time. A door slammed, there were rapid creakings, and then the sound of Randall shuffling into his gumboots. Tris heard him thumping off over the veranda and out into the day.

It felt earlier than it really was, but that was because the sun, which streamed straight into their big room first thing in the morning, was getting up a little later each day. Tris lay perfectly still, enjoying the silence and the feeling of being in bed and yet spread out through everything around him. In the distance he could hear seagulls crying on one of the little beaches that edged the peninsula. No matter how many seagulls there were, each gull sounded as lonely as if it were the last gull in the world.

He got up at last, without disturbing Tab, pulled

his old blue-jeans up and his red jersey down. He fed the hens and Bessie the goat, brought in wood from the stack on the veranda, got the old stove going, then turned on the distant generator so that washing water for the day ahead would be heated. Once again the land seemed to have a heart, beating through invisible underrunners, through the poles of the house and the soles of his feet and up into his head. Ten seconds later he no longer noticed it. Twelve seconds later, the pump began to chatter busily, water climbed from tanks under the house and trickled into the header tank somewhere in the roof. The kerosene fridge had had another disgraceful accident. A pool of water was spreading out in front of it.

There was a soft thump behind Tris. Puzzle appeared at the open window, mewing in a hollow, moaning way. Tris recognized these chilly cries, and knew, without turning round, that Puzzle was bringing some helpless prey inside so that people would see it and praise him. Turning, he glimpsed a thin tail dangling below the cat's whiskers. Puzzle had caught a mouse. Jumping from the windowsill on to a bench, he ran rapidly to the centre of the room, paused, and set his mouse down on the square of carpet. Then he crouched, staring at it with his ears forward, hoping it would run around and give him a chance to play, but the mouse was quite dead. When it didn't move, he dabbed at it encouragingly with his paw. Tab, suddenly realizing that Puzzle had prey, leaped eagerly off the bed, whereupon Puzzle snatched up his mouse once more, beginning a furious growling, as rhythmic in its own way as the growl of the generator. He glared at Tab and at Tris, too.

'I don't want it,' Tris said irritably. 'I'm having toast.' Tab hunched down, staring closely at the mouse dangling from Puzzle's mouth. Feeling impatient with such fierce feelings so early in the morning, Tris tossed Puzzle, mouse and all, out on to the veranda and shut the window firmly. Immediately, Tab leaped up on to the sill, upsetting a sprouting avocado stone in a pottery vase. Sitting as close to the window glass as he could, he peered out longingly.

Filling the woodstove kettle with water, Tris put it over the fire, which was beginning a pleasant hollow roaring inside the stove. With the sound of water overhead, and the sound of fire beside him, he began to make his school lunch with slices of Randall's home-made bread. This particular batch was rather too crumbly and Tris longed, not for the first time, for sliced bread from the shop, even though such a longing seemed disloyal to Randall, and to nature too. Grown-ups praised Randall's wholesome slices, but kids at school looked at them scornfully. 'Your sandwiches look like woodwork,' Brian Morley had once said. But then Tris remembered Winola's theory that raw food had spirits in it, and, though Randall's bread wasn't exactly raw, it certainly looked as if it might have its own spirit, too. Smiling, he spread it with cottage cheese, and then slapped lettuce and cheese between two slices.

He heard a thump on the veranda and a creak at the door. Randall himself came in looking bright-eyed and healthy. He was carrying the paper under his arm, so he had already been out as far as the gate. Tab leaped down, darting between Randall's legs.

'Any letters?' asked Tris.

'At this hour in the morning?' Randall asked him back.

'He sometimes comes early,' Tris said, meaning the postman. 'Anyhow, I'm making tea. I've got the toast on!'

'You're not only beautiful, you can cook as well,' said Randall. 'Why don't you adopt me and look after me?'

'I look after you already,' Tris said. 'Shall I grate some apple to go with the yoghurt?'

'Grate some apple?' Randall asked. 'Where do you get these ideas? God gave us apples so that we could stew them.'

'Raw food has good spirits in it,' Tris said quickly, smiling to himself. 'The spirit goes into you and makes you healthy.'

'I'm all in favour of that,' Randall said.

The apples were Granny Smiths picked from their autumn trees, out beyond the bath in the garden.

'I'll grate around the worm holes, shall I?' Tris asked. 'Or would you like the worms, too?'

'Are there good vitamins in raw codlin worms?' asked Randall. 'I know cooking them ruins their food value.'

'I think it depends if they've got dew on them,' said Tris. 'Dad, we should *spray* our trees.'

'I'm opposed to sprays,' Randall said.

'Are you in favour of worms?' asked Tris. He began grating an apparently sound apple and found a small brown worm hole running through it. 'Every single thing's got underrunners,' he complained.

'So has life!' sighed Randall, unfolding the paper. 'Great on the surface and spooky underneath.'

'Grate on the surface,' said Tris, grating a new apple, 'but watch out for what's in the core.'

After breakfast Tris got his school things together while Randall began psyching himself up for the day's work, making little darts into his office, sharpening pencils, and groaning aloud at the thought of all he had to do.

'You can get computers now that do all that sort of designing stuff,' Tris told him. 'They work it out better than people do.'

'Go ahead. Make my day!' Randall answered rather snappily. His face cleared. 'I wonder if you can get a computer that works by pedalling, or runs on kerosene. You off? Be good! Be careful!'

'You always say that,' Tris said. 'And I always am!'

'Let's keep it that way,' Randall answered. 'I'm going to finish some work here, and then this

71

afternoon I'm going to go down and get seaweed for the compost, and check the trees because I think our rabbit population might be creeping up again. And if the tide's right we could set a net later ... catch some flounders.'

'Suppose Victoria visits?' asked Tris.

'We'll all flounder together,' said his father. 'She's much more practical with fish nets than we are.'

Sylvia was not at school. Every now and then she took a day off sick. 'I have migraines,' she boasted, making herself sound important. She was lucky to be away, for Brian and Guy were in their tormenting mood – the same mood made stronger by being doubled. This mood usually seized Brian to begin with, then caught Guy about an hour later. They would start clicking their ballpoint pens, asking silly questions, yawning loudly and secretly tattooing their desk tops with their compasses. The teacher, Mr Craig, would become increasingly irritable, not just with Brian and Guy but with everyone in the class. However, when school was over Mr Craig could get away from Guy and Brian. Tris still had to walk home in Morley company.

'Hey,' said Brian, 'is it true your old man is getting married again?'

'No,' said Tris, but Guy and Brian reacted as if he had said 'Yes!'

'You'll have a stepmother,' said Guy.

'Never mind,' said Brian. 'It won't last long. She'll shoot through like your own mother. Everyone reckons your dad's a real no-hoper. No money! No car! No hope!'

'Well, at least he's got a licence!' Tris yelled back, because six months ago Mr Morley had lost his licence, and Mrs Morley or his cousin Arnie had had to drive him everywhere until he got it back again. **Councillor in Court**, the headlines in one of the community papers had said. Being reminded of this infuriated the Morley boys. They vanished between the lines of Morley fruit trees, shouting insults and threats.

Tris walked on. *'Stay cool!'* Selsey said. *'Their brains are probably infiltrated by Tangoid Talking fungi.'*

Tangoid Talking fungi, thought Tris, smiling proudly to himself! Pretty good. He thought Winola would like Tangoid Talking fungi. He began to describe them to Selsey Firebone who listened all the way uphill, and then explained them back to Tris on the way down towards the Featherstonehaugh Children's Home.

'A fungi unknown to science. The spores settle down and grow in particularly weak brains,' Selsey was telling him. *'The Morleys need instant treatment.'* 'I know, I know!' Tris answered, muttering and nodding, but suddenly there was a great burst of laughter from behind him. Something wild swooped past on his right. He was buffeted by angry, displaced air. Of course, it was the Morley twins on their ten-speed bikes, back again. They had decided to harry him all the way home. They shot down the hill ahead of him, then pedalled back up again.

73

'Talking to yourself!' shouted Brian. 'Mush brain!'

'Just like your old man!' yelled Guy.

Tris knew that he should fight the Morleys because of these insults, but he was not a natural fighter, and besides, the twins were always out of reach. Struggling uphill, zooming down, darting in, closer and closer, they dared him to attack but were ready to speed off whenever he tried. Tris put his head down and trudged on, lips pressed together, protecting Selsey, for Selsey, so powerful and strong in other dimensions, was powerless in the everyday life that held school and the Morley twins. Once, Tris made a run at Brian, but Brian evaded him easily, shouting, 'Oh! Oh! He's going to hit me. Oh, I'm *so* frightened!' At last they swooped away ahead of him and did not return. Tris suspected they were laying an ambush somewhere, but in a way they had ambushed him already. They had heard him talking to Selsey Firebone and because of this, Selsey was growing fainter, drifting out of reach.

As he came to the bottom of the hill, Tris thought about leaping the ditch, running along the Children's Home fence, and rolling rapidly in under the hollow that Winola had dug, so that when the Morleys came looking for him they would not be able to find him. But if he tried this they would certainly discover his secret path, and might even catch him, too. He was not as thin as Winola. He might stick half-way.

There were no signs of Guy and Brian or the ten-speed bicycles. Yet, as Tris stood there checking things out, both boys were suddenly on him with their usual two-pronged attack, Guy rushing in from the left, Brian from the right. Brian, the bigger Morley, grabbed the straps of Tris's schoolbag and began swinging him round and round. They circled each other in clumsy orbit, Tris staggering and trying to keep his balance, Brian, his feet firmly braced, swinging as hard as he could, while Guy darted and yapped like a little dog watching bigger dogs fight. Once, Tris almost regained his balance and grabbed at Brian, but Brian saw the danger and swung harder, so that Tris stumbled once more. The road and the grass on its edges spun round him, Guy's grimacing face flashed in and out of sight. How could a fight like this come out of nothing? Tris wondered desperately. His glasses flew off, and he thought with horror that they might be broken and that Randall would have to buy him new ones out of the car money. His feet slipped. Someone, somewhere was sneezing. Tris fell on to his knees, grazing them painfully. Then, suddenly, the drag on the straps of his schoolbag was gone. Catapulting sideways across the gravel and into the grass at the side of the road, believing the straps must have broken at last, he shut his eyes as he fell.

The first thing he saw when he opened them again were legs waving in the air somewhere beside his face. Although he felt as if he were sprawling full length, Tris was immediately convinced he was really bent in half like a safety pin. His brain was sending him wrong messages. Brain damage! Tris thought. In a flash he saw himself in a hospital bed, Randall weeping over him. Then the door opened and in came his mother. 'I came at once when I heard,' she cried. 'None of this would have happened if I'd been there to drive him home from school in the Triumph Herald.' But then he noticed that the shoes on the feet were not his shoes. The feet belonged to someone else, after all. Cries of fury were ringing in the air around him. Pulling himself up on to all fours, Tris discovered Guy rolling in the dust beside him, while, in the middle of the road, Brian was struggling with Winola. She must have pushed Guy over and then attacked Brian from behind, because she had crooked her arm around his neck, and was boring her bony knee into the small of his back. Making strangling sounds, Brian clawed weakly at her arm, but Winola was too quick and too strong for him. Tris winced with reluctant sympathy, for, many years earlier, Damon Tyrone had practised this very grip on Tris himself. He knew just how helpless Brian must be feeling.

Beside Tris, Guy pulled himself upright, looking confused. Then, rather unwillingly, he started to go to Brian's assistance. Tris, encouraged to find he was not alone, was suddenly filled with confident fury. He barged at Guy so forcibly that they both toppled over again, Guy because he was grateful for an excuse to crumple up, and Tris because he had been expecting more resistance from a Morley. Leaping back on to his feet, feeling very Selsey-ish, he found that Brian was now free of Winola, but that he was backing away from her, holding one hand over his face. Guy stayed sitting down, watching and rubbing his elbows, his mouth hanging open in apprehension. For the first time Tris understood that, when Winola fought, she fought differently from anyone at school. She meant her fights in a darker, more dangerous way than anyone Tris had ever met before. The Morleys saw this too.

'We didn't do anything to you,' Guy yelled at her, but she simply stalked over to the long grass on the other side of the road and pulled up one of the bikes.

'You want this in one piece?' she asked him. Tris thought for a moment she was going to pull it to bits in front of them.

Blood was dripping in black splotches all over the grey cloth of Brian's school uniform and Brian – Brian Morley – was actually struggling against tears of pain. A few minutes earlier Tris would have been pleased to see Brian suffer. Now, he was filled with embarrassment for Brian, because Brian liked to think of himself as tough, and because, though he was an enemy today, Brian was mostly a sort of friend. But Winola had come out of nowhere and beaten him up with no trouble at all.

'Are you *scared* of blood?' she asked Brian scornfully, pushing the bike at him so fiercely that Brian took his hands away from his face to ward her off.

He grabbed the bike clumsily, trying to prevent it from being rammed against his shins. Winola spun round on Guy, who was getting to his feet. When he saw her looking at him, he sat down again.

'I don't fight girls,' he said quickly.

'I'll bet you don't!' said Winola. She looked at Tris. 'You okay?'

'I've lost my glasses,' mumbled Tris, but even as he spoke, Winola was scooping them up from the dust at the side of the road, where they lay miraculously unbroken. She polished them roughly on her sleeve, gave them to him, then turned her back on the Morleys and stalked past the gate of the Featherstonehaugh Children's Home as if she hadn't the slightest fear of being seen and called inside. Tris stood, looking from Winola's retreating back to bewildered Morley faces – Brian dabbing at his nose, Guy standing up cautiously, now that all danger was past.

'My dad'll ring the Matron,' Guy called after Winola. 'He's a councillor!'

'Big deal!' Winola shouted back without looking over her shoulder. 'A councillor! Who cares?'

Guy threw a stone after her, but there was no real spite in it. He just wanted to feel he'd had the last word. The stone fell beside her but she didn't seem to notice it. There was nothing Tris could do but follow her. At the corner he glanced back again. Both ten-speed bikes were labouring up the road on the opposite hill.

Automatically, Winola and Tris scrambled into the grass tunnel and went on their secret way towards Tris's gate.

'They might tell the Matron,' said Tris after a moment. 'Brian was bleeding all over his school clothes. His mother will be mad!'

'I'll just say I saw them picking on you and ran out of the gate to help,' said Winola. 'I won't have to tell anyone that I tunnelled out. Anyhow, his mother should soak his shirt in cold water as soon as he gets home. Serve her right if she doesn't.'

'But won't the Matron be mad with you?' Tris asked.

'Well, what can she do?' Winola said. 'She can't complain to my mother. She can't fine me, because I haven't got any money. She's not allowed to belt me. Parents can do anything to you but the Matron's got to be kind. She could stop me watching TV, but I couldn't care less.'

Tris followed her. Now it was all over, he couldn't help wishing that he had been the one to do the rescuing. But things often turned out the wrong way round. Winola sneezed twice as they climbed the hill under the plaited screen of old summer grass. Apart from that they climbed in silence.

CHAPTER EIGHT

———— · ————

Winola watched Tris check the letter-box. Empty again. He had imagined she would leave him at the gate but, instead, she followed him through.

'Did you say there were tunnels here?' she asked him.

'Underrunners,' said Tris. 'They're called underrunners. The soil gets swollen by rain in winter, and then in the summer it shrinks and cracks, but you can't see the cracks on the surface, not until they eat their way out.'

'Eat their way out?' asked Winola, looking pleased.

'The soil on top collapses and there they are,' Tris explained. 'Underrunners!'

'Show me!' demanded Winola.

'Is there time?' asked Tris.

Winola stretched out her arms. The sleeves of her jacket seemed to creep up almost to her elbows. It was much too small for her. Tris saw her bony wrists, and the coloured fingernails like little blobs of paint on the ends of her fingers. She was wearing two Mickey Mouse watches, one on either wrist.

Tris noticed that she had inked in a skull on the back of her hand.

'Getting under the fence took one minute, fighting took three minutes!' she guessed. 'I've still got time.'

Tris looked at the watches with respect.

'How did you get two?' he asked.

'One Christmas, two brothers,' she said. 'Come on! Show me round.'

Tris led her round the road and up the slope to the biggest underrunner he knew ... the one that held his hidden stores.

'They're dangerous. They can fall in,' he explained.

'I'll just try one out,' Winola said, 'in case we ever need to hide.'

This was exactly what Tris had often thought, crawling around in these earthy caves that seemed just the right shape to hold him. He slid down first, Winola following him, and they folded themselves together into the hole, knee to knee, eye to eye as if they truly were escaped prisoners, or conspirators hiding from enemies or in search of a secret place to plot and plan.

'If it gets dangerous,' Winola said, 'this would be an *excellent* place to come. You and me ... and Selsey Firebone.' She sneezed and shook her head as if the sound of her own sneeze had tickled her ears.

'*The Veng will easily find you if you sneeze like that!*' Selsey Firebone said, and laughed. Tris and Winola laughed too, knee to knee, eye to eye, under the ground.

'I told you, I take antihistamine,' she said. 'I have some in my pocket. But it makes me sleepy when I haven't taken any for a while. I reckon it's better to sneeze than to go to sleep.'

Tris showed her his secret store of Coke and peanuts, and she smiled her wide, moneybox smile at him.

'That's really *radical*!' she said. 'If we had sleeping bags we could stay here for good.'

'In orbit,' Tris suggested. 'It's like a space capsule. The Apollo astronauts didn't have as much room as this.'

There was a sudden tiny alteration in the air around them.

'What's that sort of . . .' Winola stopped. She didn't know how to describe it.

From the moment they had climbed underground they had felt the faint vibration of the generator on the other side of the peninsula. Now it had been turned off. What they were feeling was sudden stillness.

'Is it the whatsitsnames . . . the Veng?' asked Winola. 'Cloning villains.' As she said this she let her eyes wander around the wall of the underrunner. Something about this considering glance made Tris wonder, uneasily, if the game of Selsey Firebone was true for Winola in a different way from the way it was true for him. As if she knew what he was thinking, Winola said in a low flat voice, 'He rang up and asked to speak to me last night . . . the one who's after me, that is.'

'What did he say?' asked Tris, relieved to find that it was a game, after all.

'I wouldn't talk to him,' Winola said. 'He just wants secret information from me. The Matron says he's in Wellington.'

'That's hundreds of miles off,' said Tris.

'He's got a car, though,' Winola muttered. 'Suppose he drives down here and tries to see me?'

'Don't talk to him,' said Tris.

'The Matron might make me,' said Winola. 'She doesn't know what he's like. He looks okay. He acts okay. Well, most of the time!' She glanced restlessly towards the opening above them. 'Let's get out now.'

They scrambled out of the hole. Space suddenly burst around them. 'Hey! Wonderful space! Wonderful sun!' cried Winola, beaming. She did a little stamping dance, and smiled up into the arch of the sky.

'Watch out! The underrunner'll fall in. I mean the space capsule will,' cried Tris.

'There's so much *room* here!' Winola cried into the air, ignoring his warning.

Out here, where the old sheep track ridged the tawny slope, she was a different person. Her thinness made her look lighter – as if she might take her feet off the ground and blow away. But she looked too wiry, too determined, too *powerful* to be taken against her will, even by the wind.

'Let's gallop!' she called.

And she took off, tossing and leaping along the

old road. Tris didn't bother to gallop. He just pelted after her, running in an ordinary way.

'I'm riding,' Winola yelled back to him. 'I'm riding to freedom, with the wind blowing my hair out behind.'

Though her hair was clipped short, she tossed her head just as if she really had a wild mane streaming like a flag behind her. She was horse and rider mixed into one creature. Selsey Firebone, however, was too technological to ride a horse. So Tris imagined a laser motorbike and zoomed along making gear-change and cornering sounds as he went.

'Back to the space capsule,' cried Winola at last, wheeling around through the tussock. Galloping, still galloping, she was unable to find the lip of the underrunner and Tris had to take the lead and find it for her.

They sat beside the hairy mouth of the hole with the wind in their faces. A hawk flew overhead, hovering, then wheeling away, borne up on a shaft of warm air which rose unseen from the slopes below. The geese, leading their mysterious lives up and down the tide-line, started a gabble of alarm as the shadow of the hawk passed over them.

'I could live in this hole,' Winola said. 'I could hollow it out a little bit more and weave blankets out of grass and all that! Be like Thingummy.'

'Be like Rat and Mole,' said Tris. She looked blank. Tris could tell at once that no one had ever read *The Wind in the Willows* to Winola.

'Thingummy Crusoe!' she said. 'That desert island job!'

'*Why not!*' said Selsey Firebone, and Tris found it easy, just for the moment, to believe in a Winola who lived in a hole for weeks and months and years. 'Your name could be Win-Hola,' he suggested. 'It would mean you had won yourself a hole to live in for ever after. You could be the mysterious burrowing-girl. People would catch a glimpse of you at night, flitting like a ghost. Whoooo!' He scrambled up and flitted a little himself so that she would get the idea.

'Say I got to know this place so well I could run all over it even in the dark!' she said. 'And then back to the hole. Out of sight for ever.'

But then, as she looked down into the hole, her expression changed. She suddenly put her head down on her knees. Tris watched her, waiting for some new idea, some new game, but she sat like that with her face hidden for some time.

'Are you okay?' he asked at last.

'Yes,' she answered in a muffled voice, without raising her head.

'Are you crying?'

'I never cry,' she answered proudly, though her head was still bowed and her voice muffled.

She raised her head, and indeed her eyes were perfectly dry.

'I *can't* cry,' she added, sounding puzzled. 'I used to when I was little, but now I've grown out of it.'

'Not even if you hurt yourself?' Tris asked.

'I yell,' she said, 'but I don't cry.'

Tris, however, felt certain she had been doing a sort of dry-eyed crying of her own. He tried to distract her with science fiction.

'Wherever you look there are tunnels running through everything,' he said, waving his arms at the world around him. 'Underrunners everywhere: crabs in sand and codlin caterpillars in apples. Everything half eaten and full of holes.'

'That's science,' Winola told him. 'Think down to the smallest bit of anything there is and it's mostly nothing. Even us!' She held out her hands and looked at her palms, then at her bitten nails and her two watches. 'Mostly nothing! Even Mickey Mouse.'

'We could invent a machine that would let us hide inside our own nothing,' suggested Tris. 'It would sort of turn us inside out, without hurting us. We'd be invisible.'

This reminded Winola of the odd, shapeless adventure they were telling each other. She grew businesslike.

'So we're hiding,' she said. 'They're after us, right?'

'Right!' said Tris.

'The members of B.I.C.! Like those two Veng disguised as boys. They're after you, and *he's* after me.'

'All green like frogs,' said Tris.

'Hang on! I like frogs,' Winola protested.

'You wouldn't like these ones,' Tris said. 'They're a computer-generated society that got out of hand. They spit acid.'

Winola pulled a face.

'Even ordinary spitting's pretty gross,' she agreed.

'This spitting burns holes in human skin,' said Tris. 'And they're the ones who are after us. Their leader is called Gyan.' He had just invented the name by mixing Guy and Brian together. 'He wants our secrets.'

'He invented the Veng, but he's not Veng himself, though,' suggested Winola. 'He looks zero cool, and everyone likes him. And he drives a 1969 Lotus Elan, with machine guns mounted in the headlights, and a walnut dashboard. And a sun roof.'

Tris's mouth fell open and hung open. He had been about to add to the story, but as Winola spoke he somehow lost his words. Then they came back to him with a rush.

'A Lotus!' he exclaimed nervously. 'A yellow one? I saw one of those driving around here!' He told her this in a small voice, knowing as he spoke that there must be a connection between the Lotus in Winola's story and the one he had seen two days earlier.

Winola's grey eyes swivelled in Tris's direction. It was like being picked out by a searchlight.

'Yellow?' she repeated.

'Just down the road from here,' Tris explained. 'A man stopped and asked . . .' He broke off, remembering just what it was the man had been asking.

'What did he ask?' Winola cried, taking his arm. Her thin, hard fingers dug into him.

'He asked the way to the Home,' Tris admitted.

'Did you tell him?'

'It's on all the A.A. signs,' Tris said defiantly. 'It's not a secret. And yesterday . . .'

He thought lasers might feel like Winola's blazing eyes.

'Well, yesterday I saw him again,' Tris went on. 'He was on the track out there, watching the Children's Home lawn through binoculars. But he can't be *your* one.'

'Why not?' asked Winola.

'You said he was in another city,' Tris reminded her.

'*He* said he was in another city,' Winola said. 'But he tells lies all the time.'

'Who is he?' Tris asked.

Winola didn't answer this question. She simply sat staring at him as if she were looking through him, and through the ground beyond him, too. Her gaze, he thought, could bore right through the planet earth and out into space on the other side.

'I'm not going back to the Home,' she said at last. 'Not if he's watching for me.'

'Where will you go?' asked Tris, although he already knew the answer. What had been a game was turning real even as he sat there, with the hawk far above him, and the geese below.

'I'm staying here!' said Winola impatiently.

'They'll think I've set out to walk to my auntie's house. They won't think of looking in the obvious place.'

Tris said nothing. He did not know what to say.

'That's what you do when you want to hide something,' Winola went on. 'You hide it in the obvious place. At least that's what it says in detective stories. And I'm going to hide in this hole.'

CHAPTER NINE

Tris got home and found Randall on his knees packing things into old cartons.

'What are you doing?' he asked.

'Spring cleaning!' said Randall.

'It's *autumn*,' Tris cried, fixing his eyes on the cupboard beside the shower alcove and wondering how he could get Randall out of the house for five minutes. His sleeping-bag was in the top half of that cupboard. You could live in a hole without a table and chair, but you had to have a sleeping-bag. Randall laughed and kept on packing.

'Autumn cleaning, then,' he said.

'Anyhow,' said Tris, 'you just shift rubbish from one place to another and call it spring cleaning.'

'I always think things will come in useful, and then they don't,' Randall explained, tugging his ponytail in the way he did when he was ashamed. Because he was going bald in the front it made him look as if he were pulling his hair back off his head.

'I suppose Victoria's coming?' Tris asked.

'She is,' said Randall. 'But she's being useful, not just pretty.'

Tris frowned, trying to work out whether Victoria was pretty or not.

'She's not that pretty,' he pointed out. 'Her face crinkles up when she smiles.'

'So does mine,' Randall replied. 'We almost match, but she's got better legs!' He straightened up, looking down at Tris, still tugging his ponytail reflectively. 'You think she's coming to carry me off to her lair, don't you, but if she tried anything like that I'd scream and toss my curls. No ... she's bringing her trailer round and we're going to the dump together. Dump diddledump diddle dump dump dump!' he sang. 'You are looking on some of this rubbish for the last time.'

Tris glanced sharply down at the pile of cartons Randall had assembled from somewhere. He picked up a faded toy hippo.

'Are you throwing this out?' he asked indignantly. 'It's my favourite!'

'Correction, kid! It *was* your favourite,' Randall said. 'It's been in the back of a cupboard ever since we came here. And anyhow, I'm not throwing it out. I'm recycling it. Rosie can choose what she wants from that box, and then we'll send the rest to the Social Services. Someone should love that poor neglected hippo *now* ... not just remember loving it ages ago.'

'Are you giving all my old toys to Rosie?' cried Tris angrily. 'She comes here and uses my dinosaurs and now you're giving her my hippo!' He grabbed up a battered tinsel Christmas tree from another box. 'Are you throwing this out?'

'I am!' said Randall. 'It's had its day. If we put that up at Christmas it would make us miserable.'

Tris thought of the old tinsel Christmas tree, tossed into the dump, being slowly engulfed by hedge clippings and catfood tins. He knew Randall was right; he didn't really want the tree, and yet he could not bear the thought of it being carried off in Victoria's trailer, never to return. Then, suddenly, it occurred to him that for someone like Randall, a visit to the dump in Victoria's company might be as romantic as dancing to violins.

'My mother bought this,' he cried, waving the Christmas tree like a wand, believing he could actually recall her folding its glittering arms out, transforming the dark, old city house they had once lived in with the little sparkling tree. Rainbow colours, probably from Christmas lights, had shone on the wall behind it. Then Tris saw that Randall was looking at him sadly.

'Tris!' he said gently, shaking his head. 'My best-beloved boy . . . Your mother didn't bring you that Christmas tree. Dearie from next door gave it to you.'

For some reason this upset Tris even more. If he couldn't remember his mother properly, there was no reason why she should remember him.

The rattling chug of the Volkswagen, growing louder and louder as it came down the peninsula, interrupted them and they both looked out through the glass doors to watch it arrive. It startled Puzzle out of some cat nest of dried grass, and he took off under the house, his thin tail bristling with outrage. The Volkswagen was pulling a trailer so old that Tris half expected it to shudder and fall to bits when the car stopped. Victoria scrambled out of the car with Rosie at her heels. She waved at them enthusiastically. Tris couldn't help smiling and waving back.

'Help me load up,' Randall said to him. 'That's an order!'

Tris carried carton after carton out to the trailer. He felt as if his childhood were being taken to the dump to be covered over with beer cans and plastic bags.

'What's the matter, Ratty?' asked Victoria, noticing his solemn face.

'Ratty!' cried Rosie like an echo, and signalled to him with Bombom, as if they were ships passing each other at the mouth of the bay.

'He's having second thoughts about throwing some of these treasures away,' Randall said. 'Tris, we can't hang on to everything. We have to let some of it go.'

'Don't *counsel* me!' Tris said warningly. He suspected Randall might be talking about something more than an old Christmas tree, broken heaters and faded hippos.

'Besides, you're the one who complains about the junk . . .' Randall added, pointing at him sternly.

93

'And you're the one who wants to recycle everything,' Tris said. 'We save stuff for no reason and then throw it out for no reason.'

'Those bottles will go in the bins at the dump,' Randall said. 'They've got one bin for green glass, another for brown glass . . .'

'I know!' Tris said quickly. A sharp colourful idea had come rushing into his head. 'Is Victoria coming back for dinner?'

'Yes,' said Randall. 'Want to make anything of it?'

'Don't you men fight over me!' said Victoria. 'I'll be bringing half the dinner, Tris. Fruit salad and cheese cake? We might even run to ice-cream,' she suggested temptingly.

'Unexpected pudding! Yum!' said Randall greedily.

'Yum, yummy, yum, yum!' cried Rosie, laughing as if she had said something amusing. She rolled on the floor showing her pants.

A Selsey-ish idea exploded in Tris's head. Selsey almost said it aloud, but Tris got in first.

'Well, could I ask someone for dinner too? If there's enough pudding to go round?'

They both stared at him.

'Of course you can,' Randall cried enthusiastically. 'I *want* you to have visitors. It's you that won't invite them!'

'Well, I want to ask someone tonight,' Tris said.

'Who is it?' asked Randall. 'The Morley boys?'

'Elaine Partridge,' Tris said.

Randall sat down suddenly and stared at Tris as if

he had suddenly announced he was inviting royalty to share the unexpected pudding. He wrinkled up his face incredulously.

'Let me get this straight!' he said at last. 'You've actually asked Elaine Partridge to dinner tonight? And she is actually allowed to come here? *Here?*'

'Yes,' Tris said, wishing he had made it Sylvia. However, his father had a rough idea what Sylvia looked like. 'She said she'd wear her old clothes.'

'Old clothes? Great!' said Randall a little sarcastically. 'And she asked her mother?'

'Yum, yummy, yum, yum,' cried Rosie trying to get them to giggle with her.

'Mrs Partridge said she'd drive her to the gate and pick her up at half past eight,' Tris said. 'She doesn't want to drive out along our road because she doesn't know where the underrunners are.'

'She won't even know *what* underrunners are!' said Randall. 'And I forbid her to try our road. I don't want to spend the evening trying to jack her back wheel out of some hole.'

'Not with her history of accidents,' said Victoria. 'She wrote off a new Daihatsu Charade two years ago, failing to give way.'

'Anyhow, our jack doesn't work,' said Tris.

'I'll have to shower! I'll have to get dressed up to do you credit,' cried Randall. 'Elaine Partridge. You *are* moving up in the world.'

'I'll bring flowers as well as pudding,' Victoria declared, laughing.

Tris saw that, although Randall and Victoria often made fun of the rich Partridges, they were impressed. They were going to go to the trouble of tidying up, and Randall was going to wear his old velvet jacket. They were going to do all this for Winola. His heart sank.

'You don't have to dress up!' he cried. 'She'll be wearing old stuff.'

Victoria fitted Rosie into her car seat, and she and Randall drove off to the dump, looking anxiously out of the back window at the disintegrating trailer. It was not licensed, so they would also have to watch out for any cruising traffic cop who might be keeping a watch. Tris had the house to himself. He went to the store cupboard, got out the sleeping-bag and an old sponge rubber pillow, and carried them out along the peninsula to the underrunners where Winola was waiting for him.

'You're coming to have dinner with us,' he said. 'But I said you were Elaine Partridge.'

'Nice one!' said Winola approvingly. 'Who's Elaine Partridge?'

'She goes to our school,' said Tris, 'but she's going to a private school next year. Her father's really rich. They've got three cars, and one's a Fiat X19.'

'That doesn't mean much,' said Winola. 'The one who's after me's got an awesome car and trendy clothes but nothing else. It's all he wanted, and it's all he's got.'

'The Partridges have got a house with a stone wall and a gate and a garden,' said Tris.

Winola looked down at herself.

'I'll never look like her,' she said doubtfully. 'I'll never ever look like one of those rich kids – never, never, never, never, never!'

'I said she'd be wearing her old clothes,' Tris explained.

Winola did not look altogether comforted. 'You can't just suddenly look rich!' she said. 'You have to practise.'

'It's a big dinner tonight ... pudding, too! You could fill yourself up,' Tris explained. 'Some of it might be raw,' he added encouragingly.

'Well,' said Winola, grinning. 'Thanks!'

They arranged the sleeping-bag and the pillow in the underrunner. It looked cosy, curled up like a blue nylon cocoon, and Tris felt envious. If anyone were to sleep in the underrunner it should be him, he thought. He had found it first. Then they set off through the tussocks to Tris's house. Victoria and Randall were not yet back from the dump.

'I'd better look clean,' said Winola. 'Rich kids look super-clean. I'll wash my hair, too. It only takes about a minute to dry.'

'I'll keep a look-out,' said Tris, 'but it's probably okay. It takes a while to get to the dump. Victoria's car's an old rattle-bang, and the trailer's coming to bits. They'll have to go slowly.'

Winola rolled up her sleeves. She washed her face

97

and her hair, and then borrowed the scrubbing brush to brush her clothes. Then she turned her pink-lined parka inside out.

'It's reversible,' she pointed out. 'I hate this pink colour, but at least it looks newer.' Privately, Tris thought everything Winola wore looked beaten into shapelessness, and even if she had had anything new to wear, there was something about Winola that would take the new look away from it.

As she brushed herself down and sponged spots from her T-shirt, Tris gave her vital facts about the Partridges, their cars, their aristocratic cats, and their kitchen which had a dishwasher, a microwave, and a wall oven – so you could see a soufflé rising without having to bend down. Tris had never been into the Partridge house, but Elaine had once done a project on the way modern technology was used in the home, so everyone in his class knew a lot about the wonders of the Partridge kitchen. As he talked, Tris saw Winola begin smiling scornfully to herself.

'They've got a terrific alarm system too,' he said, almost as if it were his house he was boasting about. 'It connects with a security place in town.'

'It'll probably catch my brother!' Winola replied, grinning again. 'He's been caught twice already, breaking into houses.'

'Is he in jail?' Tris asked, impressed against his will.

'Juvenile Court. Remand Home,' said Winola. 'Inadequate parental control.'

'It'll take the cops ages to get over here,' said Tris comfortingly. And then he remembered something else. 'Anyhow, the Partridges have got a German Shepherd called Butcher. Butcher might get him first.'

'I'm getting to hate these Partridges,' Winola complained. 'I've never even met them, but I know they're on the other side.'

There was no way that she could ever make herself look like Elaine Partridge. She came from another planet. Even after she had wiped the colours from her fingernails and her hands were clean, the bitten nails gave her a troubled edge that did not match the Partridge way of life. Then there was the skull on the back of her hand which would not scrub off.

'It's a sort of tattoo,' she explained. 'You do it with ink and a pin. I did it at my last school during Cultural Awareness.'

But when Randall and Victoria came into the room, Randall carrying Rosie, Winola somehow relaxed her true expression into a more childish, innocent one. When she spoke she softened her voice, and even made it a little babyish.

'Thank you for having me,' she said.

'Elaine!' said Randall. 'We meet at last. I've heard about you!'

'I've heard about you, too,' Winola replied.

He stared at her, frowning yet smiling at the same time. 'We haven't met before, have we?' he asked.

'No,' said Tris quickly.

Tris could tell that Randall had not expected anyone quite like Winola. Winola smiled and said 'please' and 'thank you', and fussed Tab, appearing perfectly at ease. Tab went into an ecstacy of purring and lay on his back, trusting her with his tawny stomach.

'Our cat is a Burmese,' she said. 'It cost a thousand dollars.'

She sounded superior, as if she really thought plain, purring Tab wasn't much of a cat. Although he knew she was just Winola, a runaway from the Featherstonehaugh Children's Home, Tris longed to stick up for his own cats.

'Our cats were dumped by people wanting to get rid of ex-kittens,' said Randall. 'They came completely free!'

Randall and Victoria had stopped off at Victoria's house and had collected flowers, fruit salad and cheese cake, and Victoria had changed out of her working overalls into newish jeans and a red sweater, but Randall looked as disreputable as ever. Since he had arrived home to find the guest already there, he did not bother to change.

He decided to make chicken casserole, which was the thing he cooked best. A delicious smell began to creep out of the wood stove.

'In our house we have a microwave and a high-up wall oven,' Winola said, trying hard to be like Elaine Partridge. But then she added. 'I like your stove best, though. I get sick of electricity. Everything in our house is electric. Our tin-opener's electric, our toothbrushes are electric, our spa pool's electric.' Tris had forgotten to mention the Partridges' spa pool, but Winola seemed to have guessed that they would have one.

'You wouldn't like a wood stove so much if you had to cut the wood and clean out the ashes,' he said.

'You don't know what I'd like,' said Winola, and this time it was Winola speaking to him, not a pretend Elaine Partridge.

For dinner they lit candles and lamps and turned off the generator so that the electric light slowly softened and faded away. Winola ate so much that Tris wondered if she were trying to fill up all the nothing she had said she was mostly made of. She ate in an absent-minded way as if she did not know what she was doing, but at the same time she got through a tremendous amount. Tris was amazed that someone as thin as Winola could find the room to put so much food.

'And how's Harry?' Randall asked. Harry Partridge was Elaine's father.

'Fine,' said Winola.

'Busy time of the year for him,' said Randall.

All Winola needed to say was 'Yes'. It was all anyone expected, but to Tris's dismay she said a lot more.

'It ought to be,' she said, 'but he doesn't get up

till lunch-time. He just lies in bed with a hangover, moaning about the government. And he's always home late because of his girl-friend.'

Victoria and Randall looked down into their dishes so that she wouldn't see how interested they were.

'What are you going to do about the gorse?' Victoria asked Randall, struggling to change the subject.

'I'll have get out and do it, that's all,' Randall said. 'I can't afford to hire anyone. I'll have to sharpen the old family slasher.' He mimed slashing down into a gorse bush. 'It wouldn't be so bad, but I need to finish this set of drawings in order to get a bit of money coming in. Sometimes I wonder if it's worth it.'

Winola looked up from her third slice of cheese cake.

'It is worth it,' she said. 'This is the most wonderful place I've ever been in.'

Randall looked surprised and then amused. 'I didn't think anyone around here thought much of it,' he said. 'No fencing, no water.'

'If God had meant us to drink water he'd never have given us whisky,' said Winola. '*My* father says that all the time. He drinks it like there was no tomorrow!'

'Have you seen our bath?' asked Tris. 'It's outside.'

'Outside!' exclaimed Winola, just as astonished at the thought of an outside bath as Elaine Partridge would have been. She followed Tris out among the marigolds. The bath sat there with the hose still dangling into it.

'You bath outside?' She looked up into the sky.

'No one can see us except morporks,' Tris said. 'Why did you tell them all that stuff?'

'I was just making up a story,' Winola said. 'I got sick of that Elaine Partridge and her amazing kitchen.'

'You weren't anything like Elaine!' Tris told her.

'I wasn't like *your* Elaine,' said Winola. 'I was my own sort of Elaine. Her father's an alcoholic. They're going to lose their money soon and she's going to have to get clothes from the Presbyterian Social Services like a lot of other people. One day they'll get back clothes they slung out when they were rich.'

'Yes, but it's not true,' Tris said.

'How do you know?' asked Winola. 'They wouldn't let on!'

Tris thought he ought to take her back to the underrunner before she said something so impossible that his father would know she was not Elaine Partridge.

'We should get back,' he said, 'in case the one that's after you is looking at our house through binoculars.'

'Yes, it's safer in the dark,' Winola agreed. 'Hey! Great dinner!'

'I'm walking with Elaine to the gate to meet her

mother,' he said to his father when they returned to the house. 'I'll take the big torch.' He did not mention that he had spare batteries in his pocket, as well as a book he thought Winola might enjoy.

The big torch played like a searchlight on the tussocks, and a few rabbits sat up and stared blindly into the light. They looked so at home there it was hard to think that they were unwelcome and needed to be poisoned or shot to protect the growing trees. At last they reached their underrunner. Winola slid into it and found the torch that Tris had already hidden there. In some ways it was fun to see his secret stores actually being used.

'I've brought you a book,' Tris said, passing over book and batteries. 'You can read a bit. But if the light gets dim, turn it off for a while.'

'Thanks!' said Winola awkwardly. 'I mean, you're a really choice guy. But listen!' She put her thin, hard hand over his. 'Promise me on the naked heart of Selsey Firebone that you won't chicken out and tell anyone where I am.'

Standing by the bath in the garden Tris had felt certain they were doing the wrong thing, but there was something serious about the way Winola touched his hand and asked him to swear this fearsome oath. He knew, without being told, that Winola touched almost nobody.

He walked home through the evening, feeling uncomfortable, then excited, and then uncomfortable again.

'*It's an adventure,*' said Selsey Firebone. '*A secret adventure!*'

'What a social coup!' said Victoria as he slid in through the glass doors. 'She was nice — different from what I expected she'd be.'

But Randall gave Tris the same look he had given Winola earlier. It was a puzzled look and a little suspicious, too, as if he didn't quite believe in what he was being shown.

'How about a game of snakes and ladders,' was all he said. 'Then Rosie can join in.'

'And then we'll go,' said Victoria.

In the candle-lit kitchen they played snakes and ladders, and it was not only restful, but kind and easy and good fun. Every now and then Tris thought of Winola hiding in the underrunner with her torch. When the siren of the volunteer fire brigade rang out over the water, he went out to the veranda and looked in the direction of the Featherstonehaugh Children's Home. It was easy to see it, for all the outside lights were on, and as he looked, he saw a tiny red light, no bigger than a pin prick, flashing on and off. He knew at once that it was a police car. Out in the night people were searching for lost Winola, and he was the only one who knew where she was. His heart shrank within him, yet he felt the pressure of Winola's hand on his, just as if she were standing beside him. I'll never sleep tonight, he thought. I've got a guilty conscience.

'Tris,' said Randall from the dim room beyond.

'Have you got something on that tiny little mind of yours?'

'No,' said Tris. 'I mean . . . if Victoria does get you, does Rosie get all my books, too?'

'Stop it!' Randall said. 'If I try to talk to you, you tell me I'm counselling you, and if I shut up, you reproach me. I can't win!'

'You say life shouldn't be about winning and losing,' Tris said.

'You've got me there,' admitted Randall. 'It's lucky I believe it. Oh well, let's go to bed and worry about it tomorrow.'

And that's what Tris tried to do. As he settled down in bed he heard the brush of gentle rain over the roof. Oh no! he thought. Rain! But because he was worn out with school and fighting and plotting and planning, and having something new to worry about, he finally did fall asleep after all.

CHAPTER TEN

—— · ——

Even before Tris woke he knew at once that it was Saturday, but a strange Saturday – not exactly dangerous, but not restful either. He lay with his eyes closed, pretending that he was still asleep. Silence stretched out all around him. The generator was still. The pump was silent. At last, he sat up and looked out of his alcove window at a land so softly bright, so calm and silent, it seemed like it had been created during the night. Morning light made everything unearthly.

Suddenly, Tris remembered just what it was that gave this Saturday its strangeness, remembered Winola in the underrunner, and the siren calling out the Gideon Bay Volunteer Fire Brigade late at night, and the red, blinking point of light that meant a police car was sitting outside the Featherstonehaugh Children's Home. He remembered the soft, seamless purr of the rain on the roof. Sitting beside his dinosaur collection, Tab looked down at him, smiling under his whiskers in the way cats do. The door was propped open, which meant Randall was out and about already. As Tris sat up, there were steps on the veranda and Randall came in, triumphant because he had found one of the nests the hens hid carefully in the garden.

'If we kept them in,' Tris said, 'we'd find all the eggs easily.'

'These are free-range eggs,' Randall said proudly. 'Extra healthy!'

'Yes, but we don't find them all,' Tris pointed out. 'And the hens mess the veranda.'

'We find enough,' Randall said. 'More than we need, really.'

As soon as he could get away, Tris ran to the under-runner. He saw the end of the blue sleeping-bag cocoon.

'*It's Selsey Firebone,*' Selsey announced into the underrunner.

There was silence. The earth's fallen in, thought Tris. She's smothered. She's died of rain and cold. But then he heard a stirring sound. The blue cocoon twisted. Looking straggly and wild, an earth spirit rose out of the ground.

'I've been awake for ages,' Winola said a little reproachfully.

'I think police were looking for you last night,' Tris blurted out. 'I saw the light of a police car.'

'They walked right past me,' Winola told him. At least, someone did. I heard someone walking around here. Whoever it was went away again.'

'Were you warm enough?' Tris asked.

'Yes,' she said. 'I was warm.' But she looked cold

– thin and cold – as she looked into his eyes out of the hole in the ground.

'It was quite nice sleeping here,' she said. 'I wouldn't mind if I was born again as a rabbit.'

'They have to be killed,' said Tris. 'They eat the trees.'

Winola was silent for a moment.

'What else lives in holes?' she asked. 'Something that nothing happens to?'

Tris thought of moles and water rats, but he knew Winola had not read *The Wind in the Willows*.

'Something happens to everything!' he said at last. Winola nodded slowly.

'There's nothing safe you *can* be,' she said at last. 'Too bad! Anyone around?'

Tris shook his head. She pulled herself out of the hole, blue cocoon and all, and sat on the edge of it beside him.

'Why do you talk to Selsey Firebone?' she asked him suddenly. Tris had to think about it.

'When I was a little kid, it seemed ages to walk home from school,' Tris said. 'I suppose I began talking to him then.'

'It's a funny name,' she said, glancing at him sideways. 'Did you ever know anyone real called that?'

'No!' Tris said, smiling and shaking his head. 'It's just his name.'

'Did you make it up, then?' she asked him.

'I just . . . knew it,' Tris explained. 'I've known it from the beginning of time.'

And indeed it did seem to Tris that the name had never been made up. Selsey had always been there. Now, it was his turn to question Winola.

'What are we going to do?' he asked her. 'I mean . . .'

His words stopped, but Winola knew what he meant.

'I don't know,' she said. 'All yesterday I really thought I could live in a hole for years. People do in the third world. You see it on TV. They live in old cars and holes and cover themselves with newspaper.'

'But you can't,' Tris said.

Winola sat and stared, sneezed once, sniffed and wiped her nose on her dirty handkerchief.

'I just don't know what's going to happen to me,' she said at last. 'I take up room. I can't be nowhere.'

'Tell someone,' Tris said. 'Tell the Matron.'

'The thing is,' Winola explained, 'she's got all these reports on my family and she believes the reports, not me.'

'Don't they tell about the enemy?' Tris asked.

'They do in a way, but they don't *really*,' Winola said. 'You've met him. Would you think he was mad? Really mad?'

Tris thought about the man with the sunglasses, and felt certain Winola was making a mistake. He was helping her because it was part of an adventure and she was a friend, not because he thought the man who drove the Lotus Elan really was dangerous.

'He seemed okay,' Tris said at last. 'Are you sure you're not ...' he remembered one of Randall's words '... not overreacting?' As he spoke he thought he sounded just like a counsellor.

Winola glared at him for a moment. Somehow she withdrew herself into the space, the private nothing, that, she said, filled everyone.

Then she spoke in a new voice, a more precise, cultured voice than her own. It sounded concerned, yet it sounded savage too. 'He might really want to make up for the past. That's what Miss Milne says ...' She fell silent, giving Tris a bitter sideways glance. 'What would you know about it anyway, living out here where everything's *excellent*.'

Tris didn't know what to do. He had spoken to Winola in the voice of someone who knew better than she did what was for her own good. Yet he was certain he was saying the right things.

'Who's Miss Milne?' he asked at last.

'The social worker,' said Winola. 'In our family there's a mother and kids and broken cars and social workers.'

'What are you going to do?' Tris asked, coming back to the first question again. They had talked themselves round in a circle. Winola shrugged, flapping the end of the sleeping-bag as if she were an angular mermaid swishing her tail.

'I wish I was grown up,' she said. 'Then I'd be all right. I mean, I wouldn't want a great job or anything. I wouldn't mind planting pine trees or digging

111

ditches. I could baby-sit for rich people's kids. As long as everyone left me alone.'

'Even your mother?' Tris asked.

Winola sighed.

'I suppose she'd have to live with me,' she admitted. 'But she falls in love and screws everything up. I'm never going to fall in love. Not that anyone would love me, but even if they did . . .'

'What about your father?' asked Tris.

Winola gave him a pitying look.

'Wake up!' she said. 'He's the one I'm hiding from.'

Tris was astounded. He could not imagine Winola having a father who owned a Lotus Elan.

'Just because he *had* me it gives him power over me . . .' Winola complained. 'Everyone wants to see us being happy together. They say some day I'll want to know where I come from, and who my relations are and all that. But I know already.'

'Don't you?' asked Tris. 'Want to be happy, I mean?'

'I can be happy,' Winola answered. She sounded as if she were defending herself against criticism. 'When we were on the hill yesterday I felt happy, and do you know why? Because . . .' But she did not quite know why either. 'I just was!' she said at last. 'Being outside! Being staunch!'

'Staunch?' Tris said the word aloud, half tasting it. He couldn't quite understand what she was getting at.

'It's what they say in gangs,' said Winola. 'It

means you're true to the gang, no matter what happens. All members of the gang are like your brothers.'

'But you're not in a gang,' Tris said. 'Who are you being staunch to?'

Winola shook her head.

'I know what I mean,' she mumbled. 'I feel staunch about something but I don't know what its name is.'

'Let me tell my father,' Tris said. 'He used to counsel people . . . he'll know what to do.' As he said this Tris saw that this was the only thing to do. Relief swept over him. This Selsey-ish game had got out of hand, but he could deliver it to Randall. Randall would take over and all would be well. Whatever shortcomings Randall might have, Tris now understood that, deep down, he trusted him.

'Are you mad?' Winola said. 'He'd just be sensible and I'd wind up back in the Home. I want to be somewhere where nobody knows where I am. I want to be nowhere. This is almost like nowhere.'

'Yes, but it isn't nowhere,' Tris pointed out. 'Not really!'

Being sensible seemed the best thing to be, but Winola struggled to explain something that was not sensible.

'Look . . . it's okay being nice, but it doesn't work! Millions of people are nice to me. Well, lots of people, anyway . . . wanting to help, but . . .' She stopped, waving her hands in the air. 'No one *can* help. No one can change things that have already happened.'

They sat there staring away from each other with nothing left to say.

'Are you hungry?' Tris asked her at last. It was better than silence.

'No,' she said. 'I'm still full from last night.'

'*You need to keep your strength up,*' Selsey Firebone said. '*You need high-energy food.*'

Winola grinned a little.

'Okay,' she said. 'You got any muesli on you?'

'I'll get some,' said Tris. 'I'll go to the letter-box first.'

As he came in sight of the gate, he saw Victoria closing it. She waved and he waved back. But she didn't wait for him, simply closing the gate, getting into her car and driving past him with a cheerful toot on the horn. Tris walked to the letter-box and looked in it, but there was nothing . . . not even any junk mail, and he realized that Victoria must have collected it already because lists of supermarket specials always arrived on Saturday. If his mother had written to him, her letter would, even now, be in the Volkswagen, bouncing out to the end of the peninsula. Randall and Victoria would not open it, but they would stand turning it over, looking at the Australian stamps, squeezing it a little to see how long a letter it might be, and guessing together about what his mother might have written.

Tris walked back to the underrunner and found

Winola sitting where he had left her, frowning to herself.

'*Watch out for aliens*!' said Selsey Firebone.

'What aliens do is to land on a planet and make it over, so they can live there themselves,' Winola said. 'All the people who are nice to me are trying to make me over so that they feel okay about things themselves.'

During the time that Tris had taken to go to the letter-box, she had been sitting trying to find a way of describing why he shouldn't tell his father that she was out here, living in a hole.

'They've got to try,' Tris told her. 'Try to help, I mean. They want you to be happy.'

'I want to live in one room on a hill like this,' Winola said. 'I want to come out and gallop around and then go back again. That's all I want.'

'*And have a lot of books,*' Selsey Firebone suggested, liking the idea of the one room on the hill.

Winola shrugged.

'I can't read that well,' she confessed. 'I mean, I love stories, but people have to read them to me. If I go on living in this hole I'd get a video.'

'You'd get hay fever in the spring from all the pollen,' Tris pointed out.

'I do, anyway,' Winola said. 'I'll never be fit for the world . . . pretty or clever or that, but I'd have a great time just being alone and galloping and watching.'

'Well, you can't live in an underrunner for the rest

of your life,' Tris said. 'I'm going home for a bit, to see if there are any letters for me. Don't come out because there are cops looking for you as well as the Veng leader. I'll tell Randall, and he'll work something out.'

'Don't tell him where I am,' commanded Winola. 'Just tell him that you might be able to get in touch with me . . . Then sneak back here when you can and tell me what he says.'

But she must have known she was really surrendering. Once Tris showed that he knew where she might be, he would be made to tell.

As he marched back over the peninsula, Tris thought about Winola, and at the same time imagined himself arriving home and finding a letter from his mother waiting for him.

Dearest Tris, it might say, *I have had a successful career over in Australia and have bought a Lamborghini. But money doesn't buy happiness. I miss you and Randall all the time. I even miss the diving-man peninsula. I realize now that I don't really want to live anywhere else, so I am coming home. The car will be coming by sea, but I will be on the next plane . . .'*

Randall would go with him to wait at the airport. His mother, loaded with silver chains and smelling of flowers, would come floating off the Boeing, standing out among the many other passengers, brushing her black hair back from her face. (Once again he corrected himself, remembering that the black hair had actually belonged to Dearie.) All the same, if his mother did come back they would be the sort of family that might be allowed to adopt a child. They could adopt Winola and teach her to read well, and she could gallop through the tussocks and have all the wild space she wanted. Yet, as he invented this new family, he found he was imagining Rosie there, and Victoria too – laughing and carrying cheese-cake out of her Volkswagen. A picture of the pole-house living room had formed in his mind, and it was just as it had been last night, but with his mother added in. Then he found that everyone in the room had a face except his mother. Everyone looked as if they belonged there and moved easily, but she alone stood stiffly, like a woman cut out of cardboard propped against a chair.

Tris paused with one hand on the Volkswagen, patting it a little as he might have patted a friendly dog. He looked across the strange assortment of half-useful things that surrounded the house and over the platform, which was partly a veranda. Often, the windows reflected light in such a way that all you could see were dim pictures of tussocky slopes, but on this occasion he could look right into the big room. He saw that Rosie had dragged a stool over to the chest of drawers and was playing with his dinosaur collection. Randall would have stopped her doing this, had he noticed. But he was standing on the other side of the window with Victoria in his arms and they were kissing so closely they looked like a single alien life form, two heads, mouth to mouth, hugging itself tightly in its own tentacles.

Tris watched. They stopped, smiled, said something to each other and kissed again. Tris walked round the house, down by the bath. He did not want to go back to Winola. He did not want to go inside again. He did not know where to go or what to do. A desperate excitement filled him. 'The worst has happened!' he said to Selsey Firebone. 'From now on I'll live in the underrunner with Winola. No way out!'

Yet he wasn't really angry. It felt more like being part of an adventure for which he had practised over many years.

There were leaves and twigs in the bath after last night's wind and rain. Then Tris looked beyond the bath and saw something else. Bessie was gone. Moving forward quickly to her goat-house, Tris found that her chain had gone too. The hole in the wood beside her doorway, through which it had been clamped, had broken. It had rotted a little, and she had pulled herself free at last. An apprehensive chill ran down Tris's spine as he looked over at the slopes beyond the goat-house. Sure enough, Bessie was in among the little trees that were part of his future freedom. She was munching busily, all the time looking at Tris. Anyone could tell that the young trees were the best pudding she had ever had in her life, and she was eating quickly so as to get through as many as she could before someone came and tied her up again.

CHAPTER ELEVEN

When Tris saw Bessie eating his birthright trees,
fury seized him. Suddenly he hated his father, he
hated Victoria who had distracted his father, and he
hated the diving man – the great strip of tussocks,
dirt, thistles and rocks on which he lived. He hated
its dry, rustling surface and the treacherous burrows
and tunnels that were nibbling away under it. His
hatred was so great that he could not hold it in. First
he ran, shouting and milling his arms at Bessie, who
watched him coming, chewing as rapidly as she
could. As he got close she sneered at him and leaped
easily on to a rock, clanking her chain and chewing
as she leaped. Tris yelled at her until he felt his face
turning red with the strain of his fury, but he could
not reach her and yelling was not enough. He threw
a stick at her. It sped fiercely from his hand, end
over end, climbing towards the top of the rock but,
by the time it hit her, its spinning and climbing had
slowed it down. It struck Bessie, but it was a feeble
blow compared with the blow Tris had longed to
strike. He had wanted to bowl her backwards, bleat-
ing with dismay, but she skipped away as if she were

enjoying herself. Tris danced with fury and then spun round and ran for the house.

His father and Victoria must have heard his shrieks of rage. They were standing nervously on opposite sides of the room, Victoria holding Rosie on her hip, desperately straightening the dinosaur collection. They looked around with silly smiles on their faces, friendly and guilty and foolish at the same time, as Tris burst in. By now he was past feeling angry about the kissing. His anger spread out, engulfing everything like lava or spilled soup, steaming and burning. He bounced across the room and swept the dinosaur collection and the binoculars on to the floor with a wild sweep of his arm.

'You let Bessie off!' he yelled at his father. 'She's been eating my trees. I hate Bessie and I hate this place. I hate you. I hate everything, and my mother hated it too!' Then he ran out through the other door, across the platform, up through the things that might come in useful some day, and into the tussocks. He had a vague idea that he was going to run away to Sydney. He even imagined the shape of the Sydney Opera House, looking like some sort of millionaire's racing yacht, rising up where the chimneys of the Featherstonehaugh Children's Home could be seen. He heard his father calling his name in a weak, worried voice, but Sydney was directly in front of him and he and Selsey ran towards it together.

After last night's rain the air felt soft and unexpectedly warm, more like a summer shower than an autumn one, thicker than ordinary air, and somehow impossible to breathe deeply. Every surface glowed, each strand of tussock seemed to shine as if it had been polished, and under his running feet there was a slight give to the earth that hadn't been there yesterday.

Tris did not know he was noticing its glitter or its beauty. He thought he was too angry to see anything much and, anyhow, he knew it was all a trap. The world was smiling a silly, guilty smile at him, but he would not smile back and agree that it was nice to be stuck out on the end of this great piece of land with a kerosene fridge and a bath in the garden. He wanted to be grown up *now*, not waiting to grow up, somewhere in Sydney with his mother, not dependent for his fortune on something a goat could eat. Running around the shoulders and the bum of the diving man he knew he was running in a great letter S, the first letter of Selsey Firebone's name.

As he turned into the last stretch of road past the place where an underrunner had broken through, he had his second shock of the day – not the shock of real life suddenly grown worse than ever, but a shock of surprise. The road was blocked by a sleek yellow car with a sun roof. There it was . . . the Lotus Elan, gleaming and grand, as out of place there as a table laid with white linen and silver dishes. Tris approached it slowly. He could see the peninsula and the hills and sea behind him reflected in dusky, semi-transparent colour on the windscreen. There seemed to be nobody beyond this reflection. The car was quite empty.

Tris knew he must warn Winola at once. He turned and scrambled up the slope, watching out for the man with the black jersey and the dark glasses. However, the slopes before and behind him seemed to be completely empty. He jogged the last few yards towards Winola's hiding place, planning to climb into the underrunner with her. He would hide too – hide from his father as she was hiding from hers. Only half an hour ago he had told her she couldn't live there for ever, but now it seemed an obvious thing to do. They would sleep during the day, only coming out at night to set flounder nets. They would be the ghosts of the peninsula.

'Hey!' he said, on the edge of the hole, preparing to fold himself down into it.

But a hand rose up out of the darkness and seized his ankle.

'Hey, yourself, Monsieur!' said the owner of the yellow Lotus, rising up out of the hole like a genie from a bottle, smiling charmingly, just as a television newsreader might smile at people lucky enough to have television.

'Surprise!' he cried cheerfully.

'Where is she?' Tris cried back, and at the same moment the man asked, 'Where is she?'

Having asked that one question, Tris found he could not say another thing. His heart had stopped.

He might be about to fall and die, motherless and nearly fatherless among the tussocks. But the man laughed.

'Snap!' he said.

Then he jerked Tris's foot viciously out from under him so that Tris toppled over backwards, and leaped out of the hole like an evil version of Selsey Firebone himself. Tris flailed around, sitting up and pushing his glasses safely back on his nose at the same time. The man loomed over him, looking about seven feet tall. He was wearing his black polo-neck jersey and a green suede jacket, patched on the elbows, and he was carrying a gun. It looked to Tris like some sort of rifle.

'Where is she?' the man repeated.

Tris glanced at the hole.

'No!' the man said. 'No longer! I was looking when I heard you coming back.'

'I left her here,' Tris said, despising his weak and quavering voice.

All around him was the familiar land of the peninsula, but the diving man did nothing to help. As for Selsey Firebone, he was not only silent. He had vanished. Tris was alone with his terror.

The man waved his gun in Tris's direction.

'Give me a clue, Monsieur!' he said. His menacing voice changed. 'I don't mean her any harm.' He sounded reasonable now, urgent, almost pleading. 'It's just that I want to know something. If I can speak to her, I'll explain things and she'll understand

. . . she'll tell me what I want to know, and it'll be over and done with.'

Tris was silent, so choked with fear he could not speak.

'Has she mentioned me?' asked the man, as if Tris had answered him, and he was answering back. 'She's a bit jittery. You know how girls are. They'll say anything.'

Tris thought that jittery was the last word he would apply to Winola. Besides, she wouldn't say just anything. She struggled to describe indescribable things as well as she could.

'I don't know where she is,' he managed to say at last. He tried to make Selsey Firebone speak for him, but that particular gravelly voice had deserted him for the moment. 'She's probably gone somewhere else.' At the same time he wondered where Winola could have run to in the last twenty minutes. The rain-slicked slopes were entirely empty.

At this moment someone shouted up to them from the road below. It was Randall, following Tris, probably full of apologies, explanations and counselling. There he stood, in plain sight, staring up at them as if he could not believe his eyes.

'My God!' Tris heard him exclaim. But the man did not hesitate. The gun swung up. He fired. Randall's legs seemed to fly out from under him. He staggered back, hit a pile of graded dirt at the edge of the road, and vanished. Tris let out a cry and began to run towards the point where Randall had disappeared. The man ran, too. Within a few strides his hand closed on the back of Tris's sweater.

'Let me go! Let me *go*!' yelled Tris, trying to hit backwards over his shoulder and run forward at the same time. The man twisted his hand in the neckband of the sweater. It tightened alarmingly. Tris gasped, and retched as he gasped. He was pulled back and hoisted up until he stood on tiptoe. His breath had been wasted with gasping and retching, and it was difficult to get another.

'Now come on, Monsieur . . . don't be difficult!' the elegant voice cried, as if Tris were a little child misbehaving at a party. All Tris could think of was that his father had been shot . . . that Randall was dead . . . that the whole world had turned upside down in less than a minute.

The grip on the collar of his sweater lessened. Tris, choking and gagging, fell on his knees beside the Lotus Elan.

'Get in,' the man commanded him. 'It's not locked.'

Tris flapped his hand in the general direction of Randall. He could not croak out a protest . . . not even a name. From the first moment he had seen the car he had wanted to ride in it, yet now it seemed like the car of his nightmare . . . the lonely road, the sleek machine and the groping claw ready to pull him in.

'You shot my father,' he croaked at last. But the man was interested in only one thing.

'I want to *talk* to her,' said the man. 'I don't want to hurt you, and I didn't want to hurt him. But he knew me. Ages ago he knew me.'

At that moment they heard a sneeze and turned to see Winola rising through the tussocks on the edge of the road. She was soaking wet and shivering in spite of the soft warm air. Her light-coloured eyes blazed at them.

'Let him go,' she said. 'He's nothing to do with us.' She walked cautiously towards them as she spoke.

'I only wanted to know where your mother is,' the man said, moving forward, forgetting Tris for the moment. 'Just tell me that and I'll be off.'

Tris got shakily to his feet.

'She's in Bidwell Street,' Winola said, staring the man straight in the eye. He suddenly moved. His arm swept out in an arc that seemed almost slow, almost lazy. All the same the blow knocked Winola off her feet. She fell sideways against the car.

'*I'm* in Bidwell Street,' said the man. 'I've come home.'

It was Winola's turn to pick herself up, staring at him as she did so. She moved her jaw a little, testing it in case it was broken.

'We can't talk about it here,' he added. 'Get in!' He pulled her towards him with his free hand. Tris, sidling off behind them, could see his fingers digging into her thin arm. Winola got into the car, scrambling across from the driver's side into the passenger seat.

126

In another moment they would be gone. Winola, with all her burden of trouble, would be swept out of his life. Tris longed to be brave and save her, but at the same time he longed to be silent and see her taken away. And more than anything he longed to be beside his father and to find him stunned and confused, bleeding perhaps, but living. Let him be alive, Tris thought desperately. Let him be safe.

Winola moved perhaps a little carelessly. The man lifted his hand again. Tris's mouth opened.

'*Leave her alone!*' Selsey Firebone said. '*Or you're a dead man.*'

Why had Selsey spoken? He had spoken against Tris's will. Yet if he had not lent Selsey a voice it would have proved he was a coward. Short boys with glasses have to try harder.

The man started and swung the gun in his direction.

'You too, Monsieur! I don't want you phoning anyone straight off.'

'My father . . .' began Tris. His voice trailed away. He began again. 'We haven't got a phone! Look! No power lines.' The man might not remember that there were such things as cellular phones. But the man grabbed Tris's upper arm in a grip that seemed to stop his leaping blood.

'My father's hurt,' Tris said again, pulling back, his voice faint and weak in his own ears. The man jerked him forward. He was too strong to be resisted.

'I can't worry about *him*,' the elegant voice said. 'It's everyone for himself in this life, Monsieur.'

He flipped the driver's seat forwards and pushed Tris into the back. Then he slid into the car himself, turning the key even as he slid. The engine started at once, and they began backing down the stretch to the gate at great speed. Tris wondered if he would be expected to get out and open the gate. He might manage to drop into the ditch and scramble downhill to the Featherstonehaugh Children's Home. But the man backed his beautiful car right through the half open gate. Tris flung up his arms, expecting pieces of wood to smash through the windows at him. But, though lichen-covered struts bounced against the polished paint of the car, the windows stayed unbroken, and they swung round in a spray of gravel. Then, at last, the car moved forward, shooting down the familiar hill, leaving the peninsula behind.

CHAPTER TWELVE

There was nothing to say. As they hurtled along, Winola stared straight ahead, just as if she were admiring the scenery and there was nobody in the back seat.

All his life Tris had wanted to ride in a car like this. Now, when he had his wish, he could only sit breathing little short breaths that did not seem to go down as far as his lungs.

The road along which they were speeding was the one that Tris travelled every day, twisting up and down over the hills like a dark serpent freckled with occasional bright scales of afternoon sunlight. At the gate of the Morley orchard, Guy and Brian Morley were doing wheelies on their ten-speeds. The car swept past them, spattering them with gravel. Tris did not turn his head. His neck seemed to have become a solid rod of iron. All the same, he imagined them gazing after the yellow car, jealous of its speed and style. He imagined they might even have recognized him in the back seat, and that they might be thinking he had encouraged the driver to swerve into the gravel on purpose.

The Lotus shot down into a dip in the road, and up and out again so quickly that Tris felt torn in two. His stomach seemed to go on flying freely towards the hilltops long after the rest of him was speeding forward again. Trees and gates shot past him. He knew them all, even though they were nothing but a continuous flicker. *Now, now, now,* said the flicker; here, gone, here, gone . . . barely present, already past. They raced through the crossroads as if there were no possibility of anything coming at them from the side. More than anything, Tris wanted to be at home, in the pole house on the platform, watched by the cats, the hawk, and Bessie the goat, with Randall, safe and sound, calling out from his study for another cup of coffee. Tris wouldn't even have minded Victoria and Rosie as well. All the things that had seemed so unbearable twenty minutes ago had somehow become lovable. Tris felt astonishment that people living within the same curve of hills could be living such different lives. Mr Morley, for example, would be quite safe at that moment. He would probably be having a beer, while Randall lay wounded, maybe even dead, among the tussocks. At the same time as Tris and Winola were being torn away from everything safe and familiar and taken — he could not begin to guess where they were being taken — Sylvia Collins would be recovering from yesterday's migraine.

There went the lordly iron gate of the Partridges' house, flanked by the two earthenware pots, geraniums sprawling out of them. The sleek yellow bonnet tilted upwards. They were climbing out of Gideon Bay.

Tris wanted to wake to find himself in bed, with Tab sitting on him. He tried dissolving reality by telling himself it was all a dream. That sometimes worked when he really was dreaming, but this time he was in a car, driven by the man who had just shot his father.

'Orson!' said Winola abruptly. She was speaking to the driver of the car. He ignored her. 'Hey, Orson!' she said and thumped him on the shoulder.

'Speak on, sweetie,' the man said. 'I'm listening.'

'This kid's not really my friend,' Winola said. She thumped again. 'Stop on the top of the hill and let him out.'

'Too late!' The man's husky voice was jaunty yet miserable at the same time. 'It's all too late, sweetie!'

'He doesn't even know who you are,' said Winola. 'It'll take him ages to walk down again. We could be miles away by the time they come after you.'

'What about it, Monsieur?' said the man called Orson.

But Tris could not take his eyes from the road. They were spinning round a hairpin bend, and, as they spun, Tris heard the sound of the tyres trying desperately to stay in touch with the tarred surface. The whole bay, sunny, soft and blue below him, the vast shape of the diving man stretching out into it, spun giddily through a half circle. It was all there, but he was being carried up out of it.

'Hey, you!' the man repeated, sounding friendly, almost joking. 'I'm talking to you!'

'Me?' said Tris. At least he thought he said it. He certainly felt his lips moving, but there was no sound. Clearing his throat, he tried again.

Winola pulled down the sun-visor in front of her. On the back of it was a mirror. Whoever had designed the car had assumed that a man would be driving this car, and that the passenger would be a woman, wanting to check her lipstick before she got out. Tris could see one of Winola's eyes, a cheekbone and a bit of hair reflected in it. She shifted, and his own face looked briefly back at him, dim and distant as if he were at the end of a long, twilit hall. I've gone pale, he thought. In the space of ten minutes he had nearly fainted and had actually grown pale, two things that often happened to the heroes and heroines in books. At the back of his mind he saw his father falling over and over down the slopes, but that picture was like something too hot to hold. His mind sprang back from it, and the memory of Randall tumbled away from him.

'My name's Orson Tyrone,' the man said. 'I'm an actor. Out of work for a bit, I must confess. It's not a great climate for the arts in this country at present.' He shot a glance at Winola. 'He knows just who I am now,' he said.

'Orson's been in ads on television,' said Winola.

In some ways she sounded as if she were boasting of his cleverness, rather as the Morleys boasted of their father being a councillor. But there was something about the reflected eye looking into his that suggested to Tris that Winola was not really praising Orson. Tris thought that, if she happened to be smiling, it would not be a friendly smile.

'Don't hassle me, Cis,' Orson said.

'Well, stop now and let us off. You could even get out of the country. You could go to Australia.'

The country of runaways, thought Tris wildly. Of lost mothers and fathers.

But the car was already swinging around another corner and then another and along the straight bit towards the craggy top of the hill.

'I couldn't afford a ticket. Every dollar I've got in the world is in this car,' the man said. 'Anyhow, you know what I want. I want to see your mother. I want to put things *right*.'

Down below them the city spread out, partly veiled in a brownish mist, although it was a fine day and winter was still to come. Garden bonfires were making a little weekend smog of their own.

Just over the crest of the hill, a terrifying thing happened. They had caught up with a busload of Japanese tourists, trundling sedately down the short, straight stretch that led to the first corner, a corner which entirely hid the road ahead. Tris waited for the car to slow down behind the bus. He had a mad Selsey-ish idea that he might fling the door open and jump out. He would fly through the air, rolling up neatly as he fell into the shallow weedy ditch on the side of the road. Then he would leap nimbly to his feet, just as heroes did on television, his face pale but grim, dusty and scraped slightly along one cheek but otherwise quite unswollen. Rather handsome, in fact. Of course his glasses would be broken, but there would be a reward and he would easily be able to buy new ones.

It was all a dream, of course. The car had only two doors, so Orson had control of the door handles. Anyway, he did not slow the car. If anything, he drove faster. Sweeping out past the bus, he hurtled straight towards the blind corner on the wrong side of the road. Of all the terrifying things that had happened, this was in some ways the worst so far, because it was the easiest to believe in. Being kidnapped at gunpoint still felt like part of a Selsey Firebone game, but coming around the corner and slamming straight into one of the Gideon Bay Transport trucks was entirely believable. Even a Lotus would crumple against the iron grilles of such monsters. He and Orson and Winola would all be mashed into catfood by the impact. In the mirror, he saw Winola clap both hands across her face, saw the reflection of the skull and her bitten fingernails. They whirled round the bend, and there, rising up the slope to meet them, just as if it were answering the call of Tris's imagination, came the biggest of the Gideon Bay Transport trucks, with Neville Bessemer's father sitting high up in it. Orson cut sharply in, in front of the bus, accelerating towards the next bend as he did so.

There was a scream as the bus-driver slammed on his brakes, and both the driver of the bus and Neville's father leaned on their horns so that truck and bus wailed in savage, surprisingly high, voices.

The Lotus's wheels slid sideways. Tris was flung violently to the right. We're going to go over the edge, he thought, terrified. We missed the crash but now we're going to fall. It's all over! Everything's over! He was flung left and then right again, as Orson over-corrected his wild line, shooting round the bend with the back of the Lotus sliding out sideways until they were actually lying right across the road, though still sliding forward. Then, at last, the car straightened. Orson drove on just as if nothing had happened. Tris gulped and gasped, filling his lungs, then holding his breath, looking into Winola's reflected eye. He thought the eye might have blinked, but there were no tears in it, only the feeling of someone warning him. Orson had acted as if he too might have a Selsey Firebone of his own living inside him . . . a Selsey Firebone who took no notice of any rules except his own, who did not care whether he, or anybody else, lived or died. Perhaps this was part of the message that Winola's eye was trying to flash to Tris through the mirror. And at that moment something else occurred to him, something he had been too confused to think about until now, something so strange and impossible it seemed to Tris that an act of magic had been performed in front of him.

The man had said that his name was Orson Tyrone. *Tyrone!* Dearie, Death and Demon Tyrone. The names sounded like solemn bells in Tris's mind. Cecily Tyrone.

Tris stared fixedly into Winola's eye, wondering about its messages all over again, remembering her expression and the way she had spoken to him when she had first looked at him through the mesh of the Featherstonehaugh Children's Home fence.

The rest of the trip downhill was frightening, but only in the ordinary way that going downhill too fast is bound to be frightening. The Lotus shot between the houses of rich people, well-painted roofs rising above established trees, children with well-brushed hair and expensive running shoes turning to watch them speed by into the city. Once into the maze of houses, Orson slowed down. He turned left and then right again. He crossed the river, roved lazily around under the willow trees, crossed the river again and turned in at a park and out the other end. He twisted right and left along streets where Tris had never been, into a poorer, unpainted part of town, then turned into a main road lined with factories and offices, and finally into a street so narrow it seemed to be more of an alley than a true street. It was almost twilight because the walls of the buildings on either side were so high. They were newish walls, mostly windowless. The Lotus emerged into a turning-space, where empty cardboard cartons beside the grille of a chained factory gate slumped across the footpath and into the road.

There, hidden away from everyone, was a house, a lean-to garage tilting against one wall. The garage door was open. There was another dingy house on the far side of the first house and what seemed to be the back of a crisp new building, made of breeze blocks and painted white, on the other. Something about the lean-to garage and the two old houses was eerily familiar. He heard his mother's voice, not complaining about the peninsula and the remote house out on the point this time, but saying with the same fierce urgency . . . 'I'm sick of all this inner-city decay! Let's get out into the country. I'm really into an alternative life style, and everyone commutes these days.'

Tris looked at the back of Orson's head and then deep into Winola's watchful eye.

Orson drove confidently into the garage. Then he took his gun from where it rested between the driver's door and his leg. He turned to Winola.

'No tricks, sweetie. Just get out and bolt the door behind us, there's a dear. I'll be listening to hear the bolt go home. And don't try anything smart, will you? Because I've got whatshisname sitting here with me.'

Winola got out of the car. Tris could see a little bit of the garage doorway in the mirror. He saw a rectangle of light, the sign of freedom and escape. Then a black lid came down over it.

'You know where the key is,' Orson called. A moment later a light came on, and he could see Winola edging back towards them.

There was a door at one side of the garage, a door that must lead into the house; she was feeling behind the boards to one side of it, just where Tris *knew* that the key would be hidden. He could have found it himself. As Winola opened the door, it let out a desolate wail.

'Out you get, Monsieur!' said Orson. Tris scrambled over on to the passenger seat and let himself out.

A dirty, shut-in, weary smell met him as he walked through into a room which held a sofa and two threadbare armchairs. There were no books and no pictures, just two overflowing ashtrays on the floor and an old Christmas calendar on the wall. Three doors opened into this room, one directly opposite the door they had come in by. This opposite door was partly open, and through it Tris could see into a dim space which he knew must be some sort of entrance hall. There on the wall were patches of colour, faint but familiar. Afternoon light was coming in through stained glass panels in the front door.

'Welcome home, Cissy! Welcome home!' Orson said. It was only when Tris saw the patches of colour that he really believed he was standing beside Cissy Tyrone in Dearie's house once more.

'Did you know it was me?' he cried to Winola.

'Of course,' she answered in a whisper.

'Why didn't you *tell* me?' he wailed, not sure why it mattered so much, but knowing it did.

'Why didn't you recognize me?' she hissed back.

Tris tested his memories again, but there seemed to be no relationship at all between the shaggy, long-haired, laughing Cecily he remembered, and skinny, brooding Winola, with her hair clipped as short as a boy's, and her slow dry smile.

'You look *different*,' he muttered.

'You look just the same,' she muttered back. 'But with glasses.'

'Speak up!' said Orson, following them. 'Weren't you ever told that it's rude to whisper in company?'

CHAPTER THIRTEEN

——— . ———

They had come into a house that had been empty for a long time. There was no feeling of anyone cooking dinner or making tea, or even breathing in it. And now they were inside, there was no feeling of any world outside. Someone had scribbled an anarchist symbol on one wall with a spray can of blue paint. The windows were made blank by old venetian blinds. Everything was velvety with dust.

Orson pressed the switch and the room was flooded with a grubby light. The overhead bulb was so low-powered that dimness was replaced by dullness. The only dust-free things in the room were a television set, a whisky bottle on the table, a glass and several sheets of crumpled, greasy newspaper beside one of the chairs.

'Home again! Home again!' exclaimed Orson, sounding really pleased and even affectionate, though Tris didn't see how he could possibly love anything about this house. When Orson opened the third door in the room and strolled through, Tris could see a kitchen sink with cupboards above and below, and a plastic bag sitting beside it. He saw Orson gather up the plastic bag and then open the fridge. Winola didn't bother to watch Orson. Her glance darted around the room, quick as an imprisoned bird, from the door frames to the window, from the window to the newspapers beside the chair. Orson grimaced and shut the fridge sharply, but a terrible smell of decaying meat reached Tris's nostrils. He felt himself shy away from it, holding his nose as he did so.

'Mince,' Winola murmured, smelling it, too, but not caring.

Instead, she had begun to look at Tris with an alert, urgent expression, apparently signalling some message, though he had no idea what it could be. Orson was taking milk and biscuits from the plastic bag and setting them out on the work-top.

'Dearie always was a dreadful housekeeper,' he declared.

'It's probably *old* mince,' Winola said. 'We got taken away so quickly, the social worker probably forgot to check the refrigerator. And I'm starving.' She nodded urgently at Tris.

'I am, too,' he echoed obediently, though the thought of eating anything made his stomach turn.

'That's three of us then,' Orson said with a sigh, coming back into the room, carrying his gun almost casually. 'Dearie hasn't left us a thing to eat.'

He swung the barrel of the gun towards Winola, not really aiming at her, using it almost like a teacher might use a pointing finger to single someone out. Winola looked back blankly, as if he were asking her a question she was unable to answer.

'She was a bloody awful housekeeper,' Orson repeated. 'She just didn't care.'

'We could have fish and chips,' said Winola in the same absent-minded voice.

To Tris's astonishment, Orson seemed to brighten.

'Yes, fish and chips!' Tris said quickly, hoping that he too sounded enthusiastic. 'Great! I'll go!' But he was not fooled by his own voice and nobody else was, either.

'You stay right where you are, Monsieur!' the man said, laughing. He looked at Winola. 'I mean, great idea, but there's just one problem, right?'

'It's not much of a problem,' said Winola. 'Lock us in the bathroom, and then you can go and get fish and chips from round the corner. It's the best fish-and-chips shop in town. Even yuppies stop off to get fish and chips there on their way home from work. They sell tartare sauce and lemon juice, too.'

Orson walked across the room and through the hall door. Winola watched him, looking as sharp as if she were at the start of a race waiting for someone to say, 'On your marks!' Winola was on her mark and ready to go. Once again, her eyes darted around the room, up into the corners of the ceiling, down at the sad carpet, over at the calendar. Anything, anything, Tris felt, just might turn into something Winola could use to help them escape. But Orson came back into the room, still carrying his gun casually over one arm.

'All right. That checks out!' he said. 'Come on, you two! Sorry about this, but a man's got to do what a man's got to do.'

The hall into which they passed was patched with ghosts of colour so faint they were only visible to those who knew where to look for them.

'Boss and Moddom!' Orson announced. 'The bathroom awaits you.'

Tris followed Winola into a dingy bathroom, with curling brown linoleum and cracks in the ceiling.

'Hey!' called Winola as the door closed. 'Two pieces of fish. Two each! And tomato sauce.'

Orson said nothing. The key turned in the lock. They heard a rattle, and a scraping sound.

'Blast!' said Winola softly. 'He's taken the key.' Footsteps retreated. She listened intently until she heard the front door open and close sharply.

The room held a bath with a shower over it and a lavatory with the seat closed. There were two narrow skylights high in the wall, but no real windows.

'I thought he might leave the key in the lock!' she said fretfully. 'We could have pushed it out with something and fished it back in under the door. I've seen them do that on television.'

'Yeah, you feed a piece of paper out under the door,' Tris said, 'and push the key out so that it drops on to the paper.' This was just the sort of thing Selsey Firebone knew. 'Is he really your father?' he asked, surprised to find that now, when the danger had retreated a little, his knees and hands

143

were shaking much more than they had shaken when he was in the same room with the gun. He was floppy with relief now that Orson had gone.

'Yes,' said Winola. 'We ran away from him ages ago. Tod was seven, Damon was two and I was a baby. Every now and then things go badly for him . . . not just ordinary bad, but *badly* bad . . . and then he comes looking for us. He thinks we can go back to some happy time he remembers before I was born. It never works out. My mother had to have a court order telling him not to come near us last time. She rings up if he bangs on the door, and the cop car comes round. But cops think it's a big fuss about nothing.'

'He shot my father!' cried Tris, the horror of Randall's fall making him close his eyes. But even behind closed lids he saw Randall stagger back all over again.

'He won't have killed him,' Winola said awkwardly. 'Orson's not a great shot or anything. I mean he might hit something if he was really close up to it, but not when he was firing from a distance.'

'He might have killed him by accident,' Tris cried. Randall fell, and then fell all over again, a sort of video replay in his memory.

'You usually get bowled over by a bullet,' said Winola, as if she had been shot many times. 'See, it smacks into you at the speed of light or something.'

Tris remembered something Randall had told him as they sat waist deep in warm water in the outdoor bath, looking up at the stars.

'Nothing goes as fast as the speed of light,' he said.

'Speed of sound then. Sound! Who cares?' cried Winola grumpily. She was already standing on the lavatory seat, stretching up to the slats of glass in the skylights. She could reach the bottom one with her finger tips. 'What could we break it with?'

'Why's he doing it?' Tris asked. Winola gave a noisy sigh and jumped off the lavatory seat.

'Because!' she said. 'He wants to find my mother. Because it's something he *can* do.'

'Where *is* your mother?' Tris asked.

Winola looked shifty. 'I'm not telling,' she said. 'Not even you.'

'Is she sick?' Tris said.

'She gets so unhappy it's like being sick,' Winola said, squinting up through the glass slats. 'Nothing's worked out.'

'Is he mad?' asked Tris, shivering and shaking.

'He's a real flake,' said Winola. 'You have to know what to say to him. Like I saw that newspaper on the floor out there, and I knew he'd want fish and chips, because he thinks it makes him seem like a good-fun daddy!' She began prowling round the bathroom. 'Don't get him excited, right? He's not totally drunk or anything, but he's had a bit. That's what sets him off. If he starts arguing, let him rave on. Sit there and let it . . .' she waved her arms in the air, 'just rattle on by.' She stopped, thought briefly and added, 'Don't agree with him too much, either. If you agree with him too much he thinks you're not trustworthy.'

'Are you *really* Cissy?' asked Tris.

'Yes,' said Winola. 'Well, I used to be. Cecily Tyrone. Winola's my second name. I recognized you at once.'

'I remembered the stained glass when I saw you,' Tris said. 'I mean, I remembered colours. I didn't remember what they stood for until I saw the hall. Then it all came back to me.' He could see Winola was not concentrating on what he was telling her – that she was still trying to work out a possible way to escape from the bathroom.

'You used to like those colours when you were a little kid,' she agreed. 'I remember you touching them, and then looking to see if your fingers had colours on them.'

'What happened to Tod and Damon?' Tris asked.

'Damon's in a Remand Home, like I told you,' said Winola. 'And Tod . . . it's funny about Tod. Do you remember how we used to call them Death and Demon?'

Tris nodded. 'Yes,' he said, triumphant at remembering at least one thing from those long-ago years.

'He's dead. He wrote himself off in a motorbike crash last year,' Winola said. 'That's why it's important to know what your name means. If it's the wrong sort of meaning you can get in first! Change your name. I don't want to be called Cissy!'

Tris sighed. 'How do we get out?' he asked at last. Winola looked up at the skylight again.

'If we could break it,' she said, 'we could knock out the bits of glass, and I could stand on the bog and then you could stand on my shoulders . . .' But she didn't sound as if she really believed this would work. 'We need something to reach up with.'

'Could we take the lock off the door?' Tris asked.

Winola thought it was worth trying. She took hold of the door handle and rattled it.

'We haven't got a screwdriver!' she said. 'Have you got five cents?'

Tris only had his lucky Japanese coin. The screws holding the door handle were sunk deep, and had been painted over several times. When they tried to turn them the coin slipped out again and again, chipping the thick paint around them.

'It would work on television,' said Winola discontentedly.

'Or in a book,' Tris agreed. 'It would work for Selsey Firebone.'

Winola sat down on the lavatory seat once more.

'The first time I heard you talking to Selsey Firebone, you were sort of calling to him: "Selsey! Selsey Firebone!" Like that.' Winola smiled. 'I thought you were calling me.'

Tris looked at her in astonishment.

'Selsey Firebone . . . Cecily Tyrone!' she explained. 'It sounds a bit the same when you're going mumble mumble. And when you were a little kid that's what

147

you used to call me ... Selsey was your way of saying Cecily.'

'Why didn't you *tell* me,' asked Tris, 'when you knew who I was?'

Winola shrugged.

'I don't know,' she said. 'I suppose I thought I might have turned into someone different. Sometimes it seems as if something magical will happen and I'll be someone different for ever after. I mean, I know it won't, but I go on thinking it might.'

'Maybe you could be adopted into a different family . . .' Tris said, rattling the door. It was old-fashioned and strong. Winola began drifting around the bathroom again, picking at the peeling enamel on the bath, then opening the bathroom cupboard. Tris could see shelves of ancient medicines. Selsey Firebone would have torn the hand-basin out and smashed through the door with it. But Selsey was not here. He was slowly turning into Cissy Tyrone . . . into Winola herself.

'I'm not pretty enough to get adopted,' Winola was saying. 'It's like kittens ... you can give them away when they're little and cute, but not when they've turned into cats and stop playing,' she added, taking out a bottle and shaking it hopelessly.

'We need a drug that's powerful enough to knock out an elephant in a second,' Tris suggested. Winola shook her head.

'Cough medicine from years ago!' she said. 'We never ever threw medicine away. This is vintage cough medicine.'

'*Someone* might adopt you,' Tris said. 'Someone who didn't care if you were pretty or not.' He couldn't honestly say that Winola was pretty. He knew she would not believe him if he tried.

'No!' said Winola. 'And anyhow, I have to be loyal to Dearie, and stop him getting revenge on her.'

'What for?' asked Tris.

Winola shrugged.

'I don't know!' she said. 'For running away from him. Or just for being so pretty and then getting keen on other guys. Or because they got keen on her. Half the time I'm glad to be all skinny and ugly. Come on! Help me! Think of a way out.'

Tris thought. 'Who lives next door where we used to live?' he asked. 'We could make a terrific noise. We could break stuff and shout.'

'No one lives there!' said Winola. 'It's been turned into a factory, and the rest of this dump will be bulldozed in about a year. The Nortons' house is still there, but they're old . . . and anyhow, Damon used to break into their place and pinch money. They're scared of us. You know!'

But Tris didn't know. No one had ever been frightened of him.

'My mother didn't like our house when we lived next door,' Tris said. 'But she didn't like it here *or* over the hill!'

'Didn't like it over the hill?' cried Winola. 'Why not?'

'She said it was too romantic,' said Tris. 'When

149

we lived here, she wanted to get out into the country. Then when we got out there, she didn't like the space and the wind.'

Winola stared at him.

'You live in the best place I ever saw!' she said. 'It's the space and the wind I like.'

As she shut the door of the medicine cupboard, Tris tugged fretfully at the towel rail. It wobbled. He wrenched at it fiercely and it came off in his hand. Tris and Winola stared at it in amazement. Selsey would use it to club Orson to the ground, Tris thought, and then remembered that, after all, Selsey was just Winola who had looked after him when he was little and defended him from Damon.

'We could smash the window with this,' he said.

Winola seized the towel rail. She grabbed one of the fallen towels from the floor.

'Put this over your head,' she cried urgently, leaping on to the lavatory seat, and draping her own head in the other towel. She struck wildly at the skylights with the towel rail. Glass splintered. She struck again and again. Tris felt flying shards hit the towel softly. There was a moment of silence.

'What do you reckon?' asked Winola doubtfully. Tris looked up from under his towel. Where the skylight had been, gaped an open oblong mouth, full of jagged transparent teeth.

'We might be able to slide out,' Winola said. She beat along the bottom frame of the skylight. The longer teeth splintered and vanished.

'Give me a turn,' said Tris, scrambling up beside her. It was difficult to strike upwards with the towel rail and impossible to get rid of all the glass.

'I'll check it out,' said Winola at last. Leaning on his shoulder, then grasping a pipe that ran down the wall, she scrambled up on to the cistern behind the lavatory seat and stood there, balancing uneasily. Looking through the gap they had made, Tris could now see the glaring white side of the new building that stood where his old house had been. There was not much room for anyone to slide out, but Winola was so thin that Tris imagined she might just do it.

Grabbing the towel from his shoulders, she tossed it over the lower part of the window frame, then reinforced it with her own towel as well as she could. She leaned over from the top of the cistern, gingerly sliding her head and shoulders out through the gap.

'It's not all that far to the ground,' she reported back. 'I reckon I could slide forward and then just topple out. Can you hold my legs so they don't sort of crunch against sharp bits?'

'I'll try,' said Tris, taking hold of her ankles.

'When I'm outside I'll be able to help you out,' she promised.

At that moment they heard the front door open. Orson was back. They heard his steps, which seemed slow and leisurely as if there were a lot of time, and then smelt the unmistakeable smell of fish and chips.

'Hurry!' cried Tris, as Winola wriggled desperately but gingerly forward. Her ski jacket snarled in what

151

was left of the glass teeth in the upper part of the frame.

Tris heard the key turn in the lock. Winola wriggled and gasped. The waterproof fabric of the jacket parted and white padding bulged out. The door opened.

'Dinner is served!' Orson announced.

Then, suddenly, Tris found himself knocked sideways with a blow as fierce as he thought the kick of a horse might be. He flew off the lavatory seat, somehow striking the wall with both his shoulder and his ear, and felt as if his head were shot through with arrows. From a distance he heard the sound of a struggle, and when he could see again, found that Orson had pulled Winola back into the room. She was glaring at him, breathing hard, as if she expected him to kill her at any moment. Her hands were crossed on her breast.

Orson clicked his tongue reprovingly.

'Silly girl, sweetie,' he said. 'That's not the way to go!'

Winola relaxed a little at these words, opening out of herself once more. Tris saw that the front of her jacket was covered with blood.

'I got six pieces of fish,' Orson said. 'I couldn't possibly eat all that, could I? Get out there, both of you.'

Tris picked himself up. His ear was sore and burning. He realized it had struck the edge of the hand-basin. Winola uncrossed her arms and clasped her hands together as if she were praying. Trickles of blood ran swiftly down her wrists. Silently, they left the bathroom side by side, with Orson following.

'Hey! Sweetie and Monsieur!' he said from behind them. Winola stopped but did not turn around. Tris copied her. 'Try another stunt like that and you'll be really sorry!' Orson said. 'I haven't got anything to lose, have I?'

CHAPTER FOURTEEN

There was a clock on the mantelpiece, but it had stopped. Time had stopped with it. In his made-up stories Tris could take command so that he and Selsey Firebone were always winners. But this story was beyond his control. He could only flow along with it.

'This is nice,' said Orson. 'Fish and chips. No dishes. Reading, too, if you like old news.'

As he unwrapped the paper, steam, rich with the smell of frying, rose around them, making last year's calendar rustle feebly. Orson looked up, then relaxed.

'Eat up!' he said. 'While it's still crisp.' He glanced at Winola.

'Nice to be home, Friendly Princess?' he asked.

Winola, caught in the act of licking her bleeding palms, paused and then actually grinned. Tris saw her fox's teeth, stained with her own blood. Although he knew she was just Winola, he felt a shiver begin somewhere in his head and run down his back and out into all his other bones.

'What do *you* think?' Winola asked. She must have

grabbed hard at the lower part of the skylight frame as Orson pulled her back into the bathroom. Long shallow slashes ran from her palms to her finger tips. 'Have you got a handkerchief or something on you?'

'This is all your mother's fault,' Orson grumbled, ignoring her interruption, and passing her a cream-coloured handkerchief as he spoke. Tris thought it looked like silk.

'Thanks,' Winola said casually, and began clumsily wrapping it round her left hand. The bandage slipped. She dropped her hands out of sight, frowning over her own first aid.

'I'll do it,' Tris offered, but she shook her head.

'All I want is a chance to explain myself,' Orson said, leaning forward across the table. 'Don't give a dog a bad name and hang him, sweetie!'

'Did someone tell you where I was?' Winola asked, looking up briefly.

'All my own work!' Orson explained. 'I went round to that foster home they sent you to last time. No luck.' He squeezed tomato sauce on to a corner of the paper and dipped his fish into it. 'Then I thought of the Gideon Bay place.' He nodded cheerfully at Tris. 'You know, I'm actually related to that family,' he said. 'The Featherstonehaughs-that-were, I mean. If I had my rights I'd probably own that whole damned great mansion, except that old Featherstonehaugh left it as a Children's Home.'

'Tyrone's an easier name to say,' Winola pointed out calmly.

'True,' Orson agreed. 'Tyrone is a kingly name. Anyhow, I rang up and asked if you'd been placed there.' He leaned back, quite pleased to explain how clever he had been. 'And they said they weren't allowed to give information. You know, the usual official guff . . . told me to inquire at the secretary's office over in the city. But I just knew there was a high probability that you'd wound up there. So that's when I set off with my faithful binoculars to see what I could see. And that's when I met Monsieur, here.' Orson stretched across the table, and ruffled Tris's hair with greasy fingers, pretending to be a kindly uncle in a television advertisement. Tris shrank under his touch, but tried to hide his fear by sitting straighter. 'I watched the place from all angles but . . . no sign of you. I rang up again, and asked to speak to you once, just on spec!'

'I didn't want to talk to anyone,' Winola said.

'Sweetie, I understand that. I know I haven't been the perfect father. I'll make it up to you some day, I promise. Anyhow, I was about to go down south and see if you hadn't wound up with some of Dearie's relations in Dunedin. I swung the glasses for one last look at the lovely view. And lo and behold . . . there you were, frisking about on the hillside with Monsieur. I couldn't believe my luck,' he added. 'There she is! I thought. That's my girl. Fortune favours the prepared mind.'

Winola sat, apparently considering this. She had

tried running from a dangerous place to a safe one. Instead, she had run from safety into danger.

'I'm thirsty,' she said abruptly. 'Shall I make a cup of tea?'

'There's milk and biscuits in the plastic bag,' Orson said. 'No tea, only coffee . . . instant coffee at that, but we're not entertaining, are we?'

Winola went into the kitchen. Orson watched her as she put on the kettle. Tris didn't want to sit staring at Orson across the stained newspaper and soggy, cooling chips. He could see Winola taking a packet of biscuits out of the plastic bag, her right hand bandaged in her own dirty handkerchief, her left one in Orson's. Tris stood up.

'I'll help you,' he offered. 'You might get blood on the biscuits.'

He walked boldly across the room without looking at Orson.

'Okay! *You* put them on the plate,' Winola said, as he came up behind her. The biscuits were chocolate ones, each in its own little nest of plastic. Winola opened the cupboard over the sink, produced a plate with roses round the edge of it, and three thick pottery mugs.

'I *remember* this plate!' exclaimed Tris, staring at the roses. Winola nodded silently, and began dusting out the mugs. Tris was pleased to see she used her silk bandaged hand, not the other one. Blood trickled from under the silk and ran busily down to the left-hand Mickey Mouse watch.

157

'Cissy ... I'm *not* the villain you think I am,' Orson declared in the room beyond. There was an unexpected whining note in his elegant voice. Tris thought he sounded like a spoiled child asking for something it couldn't have. 'I do love you. I always loved you kids. But your mother would make an angel flip.'

Winola gave a snuffling laugh, and looked sideways at Tris. In stories, people read other people's expressions and knew what they were thinking, but Tris could not read Winola's. Was she warning him? Reassuring him? Telling him not to try anything dangerous? She made a little gesture with her hand. Tris shook his head.

She patted the electric jug.

'Cool, man!' she said. 'Stay cool!'

'*Talk* to me,' Orson cried from the room behind them. 'Tell me what's been happening to you ... how you're getting on.'

'I'm okay,' Winola said. Tris spaced the biscuits carefully so that he could see the roses in between them and, as he did this, he saw Winola lift the edge of the dirty handkerchief. Three bright blue tablets slid out into the mug beneath. Those must have been the ones she had in the pocket of her jacket. He guessed she had tied them there as she wrapped the handkerchief around her hand. Looking at him again, she gave him an ominous Selsey-Firebone-Cissy-Tyrone moneybox smile. When she was little she had had long hair that fell down her back and a fringe that came down to her eyebrows. How had shaggy, giggling Cissy turned into skinny, silent Winola? But, after all, she had also changed into Selsey Firebone.

The kettle began to boil. Winola spooned coffee into the mugs. She put two heaped teaspoonsful into the mug that had the blue pills in it. Pausing, she looked furtively at Orson, and then added another half teaspoon.

'You're too young to understand,' Orson was calling wearily. 'I don't *want* to be like this. I want to be the way I *really* am.'

'Do you still take sugar, Orson?' asked Winola. 'Black coffee with sugar?'

When she spoke, she used the same patient flat voice that Tris's grandmother used when she spoke to his father. 'I'm only talking to you because I have to,' that flat, tired voice was saying.

'To hell with this Orson business!' said Orson. 'Call me Dad!'

'You used to make us call you Orson,' she said.

'I can change my mind, can't I?' he answered her. 'I *need* my family, sweetie. I need it to get over everything that's happened to me and to start again. There'll be a better, brighter day tomorrow.'

Winola had found old crusted sugar in a blue bowl in a cupboard over the sink. She put a big spoonful in Orson's mug. Tris saw her stirring it. Then she began crunching the spoon up and down.

The blue pills were slow to dissolve and Winola was breaking them up.

'If you let Tris and me go,' she said, 'we'll just walk off and say nothing. We'll pretend we hitch-hiked over here to get something from the old house. You can drive back to Auckland. No one will ever know.'

'You haven't been listening to a word I've said, have you?' Orson shouted, suddenly thumping the table with his fist. 'And anyhow, aren't you forget-ting something? I picked off that innocent bystander back there.'

Winola carried Orson his coffee. Tris came after her with the plate of biscuits.

'I put plenty of sugar in it,' she said.

Orson tasted it. 'By God, you did!' he agreed. 'You must think I need sweetening. Never mind. I like things sweet.' He added whisky to his coffee, and then put his arm around her. Winola did not pull away. She looked down at the top of her father's head. Her fox's teeth gleamed. She was smiling but, as she moved back to her own chair, Tris saw it was a savage smile.

'Dearie!' Orson said the name as if it was an an-nouncement. 'Come on! Where have they put her?'

'I don't know!' Winola said. 'She's in hospital somewhere.'

Orson laughed. His blue eyes crinkled at the corners but their deep blankness remained unchanged.

'Come on, Friendly Princess!' he said. 'Give me a

break. All I want to do is to talk to her. I want her to understand that it's all in the past. I love her. I really love her.'

'I remembered you like sweet, strong coffee!' Winola said. 'Would you like more sugar? There's some left.'

Orson tasted the coffee again.

'This is fine!' he said impatiently. 'Well, it's the worst coffee I ever tasted, but apart from that it's fine. Wouldn't you like things to be the same as they used to be?'

'Well, I reckon they weren't ever that great,' said Winola.

There was a silence.

'If we didn't get second chances what sort of life would it be?' asked Orson at last. 'So we don't get things right the first time round! Does that have to be the end of everything? I mean, for God's sake, tell me, has she got someone else?'

'No, no!' cried Winola. 'No! Promise. No.' Something dangerous had come into the room. Tris could feel the danger.

'May I have a biscuit?' he croaked suddenly, pushing the words out, trying to make them seem normal and polite. It felt like the bravest thing he had ever done.

Tris had been silent for so long that his voice startled Orson. He snatched up the Lee Enfield, then realized that it was only Tris who had spoken. The barrel of the gun dropped again.

'S-sorry,' stammered Tris. The fish and chips he had eaten felt like a clenched fist somewhere in his chest, pushing hard against his ribs just where he imagined his heart to be. 'I only asked!' he mumbled. Tris had hoped to divert Orson from dangerous thoughts, and Orson had been diverted. Slowly, he relaxed and smiled, then he laughed and shook his head, laying the gun beside the table again.

'He only asked,' he said, smiling. Then he looked back at Winola and his smile faded.

'Just tell me where she is,' he said in a plain hard voice, without any of the earlier light-hearted affection. 'Tell me, now!'

Winola hunched herself forward, wrapping her long thin arms around her body as if she were hugging herself. She ducked her head.

'I'm going to be sick,' she said. She suddenly went limp and toppled sideways out of her chair, falling heavily to the floor where she lay curled up, more like a hedgehog than any person Tris had ever seen before.

'She's fainted,' Tris said, getting up to go to her.

'Sit down,' Orson ordered. 'She's putting it on. I know her.'

He looked down at Winola scornfully, but doubtfully, too. Then he added more whisky to his coffee and drank, grimacing as he did so.

For a long time nobody said anything. Winola lay without moving, and Tris watched Orson, half hoping to see him fall, poisoned, on the floor. However, he had only drunk half his cup of coffee. The blue eyes watched Tris intently for a while, but after a while they grew vague. Tris imagined him setting out his thoughts like playing cards. He yawned. He yawned again. His eyes left Tris and began to wander restlessly. 'I wouldn't really do her any harm, you know,' Orson said suddenly. 'But she's so bloody stubborn. Anyone would think I was the villain of the piece.'

'Winola?' asked Tris, trying not to look at Winola lying on the floor.

'No! Dearie!' Orson said. 'Dearie!' He thumped the table lightly as he said the last word.

Tris saw it written in black and underlined as if it were printed in the air before his eyes. Scraps of Selsey Firebone conversation formed in his mind. 'Beauty's only skin deep . . .' he began, which was something he had heard or read somewhere, but he couldn't finish the sentence in any way.

'Look, shut up will you?' Orson muttered. 'You talk too much.'

So then they both sat there, neither moving nor saying anything. Orson dunked biscuits in his tepid coffee, eating them without pleasure or appetite. Tris, who hated the idea of rabbits being poisoned, even though they nibbled the trees, caught himself hoping that Winola had poisoned her father and that the poison would act quickly. He imagined Orson lying on his back with his arms and legs curled in like a dead fly. But perhaps he had not reached the poison in the coffee yet. He was just thinking this when Orson actually swallowed the last of the coffee, pausing and looking down into his mug as if the last mouthful had tasted unexpectedly bitter. Apart from that he didn't seem anxious or suspicious. Though the hands on the clock were not moving, Tris moved them on in his mind: ten minutes, twenty minutes, an hour.

Since it was the most frightening time in his life, it should have been the most exciting. But though Tris was scared, he was also bored – bored with watching Orson behind the table and Winola on the floor, bored with the room and the clock that did not move, bored with being frightened. Orson's eyes glazed over, his head nodded and jerked again. 'God, I'm tired,' he said.

Tris did not answer. They sat on and on. Suddenly, it seemed to Tris that the night began to quiver with many subdued sounds. Had the sound of the traffic crept closer? Was that a car out in the street beyond . . . more than one car, perhaps? He felt, rather than heard, a rapid rhythmic beat – not unlike that of a generator – and imagined the underrunners following him, searching for him, twisting all the way under the hills to plait themselves in and out of the wiring and drains and other hidden underrunner systems that kept the city going. He couldn't tell whether Orson heard these noises or not . . . possibly not, for Orson was looking bewildered, not just tired, but tormented. Another ten minutes and then another ten!

'A family's got to stay together,' Orson said suddenly out of the blue.

'You shot *my* father,' Tris said.

'Yeah — well!' the man replied heavily. 'Sorry about that, Monsieur. It changes everything, too. I mean, if you've done it once, you've got nothing to lose, have you?' He seemed to listen, to *struggle* to listen. Then he did something chilling. He picked up the gun and pointed it at his own head, squinting down the barrel like someone looking into a peepshow.

'I can see the future,' he said in a playful voice.

If he did shoot himself, Tris and Winola would be free to walk out unharmed. Tris longed for it all to be over and done with. He opened his mouth.

'Yes, Monsieur,' said Orson, struggling to keep his blank blue eyes open, 'you *may* have another biscuit.'

'Don't do that!' said Tris in a voice so muffled he could not hear the words himself.

'Speak up!'

'Don't do it!' said Tris.

'Don't do what, Monsieur?'

'Don't do anything!' Tris said.

'It just goes on and on and on and never changes,' Orson said vaguely. 'To tell you the truth, I've had enough! Haven't you?'

Tris thought he had had more than enough. Yet all the same . . . 'I don't want to see anybody hurt,' he said, in a soft voice — the opposite of the one Selsey Firebone would have used.

Orson leaned across the table towards him.

'Look away, Monsieur,' he whispered, and then laughed.

Tris took a deep breath.

'I don't want anyone to *be* hurt,' he said. 'I don't want . . .'

He looked down at Winola and saw blood soaking through the handkerchiefs wrapped round her hands. She lay still, face downwards. It occurred to Tris there was heroism in her stillness and patience. Patience, not action, might be the true bravery of Selsey Firebone.

'I'm so tired,' Orson said, tilting his head back, smiling, and peering down the gun barrel again. 'At the end of the tunnel something bright and small twinkled like a tiny star,' he said in the voice of someone reading to a child. Tris *knew* those words: he remembered where they came from. 'What can it be?' Orson was asking, still smiling, still peering. 'It's too glittering and small for a glow-worm!'

'*It was the water rat,*' said Selsey Firebone.

This was to be the last time Selsey spoke through Tris. His voice was gritty but trembling, too. Tris felt tears flood out of his eyes, but they seemed to be Selsey's tears. They were not tears of fear. He felt as if he were the water rat looking at Orson and seeing something hurt and ruined. An odd thing happened. Orson looked up, saw the tears. The blankness behind his eyes disappeared.

'The water rat!' he repeated.

'I'm the water rat!' said Tris. 'I get called Ratty.'

'Did your mother read that book to you, too?' Orson asked.

'My father!' said Tris. 'Ages ago.'

'And now you're the water. rat looking back at me?' Orson asked. He was amused, and for the first time genuinely friendly. 'I want to sleep and never wake up,' he said aloud to the dismal room.

At that moment there was a knock on the door. It was a definite knock, but not loud or demanding.

'They're out there, you know,' Orson said.

Suddenly the night vibrated with a huge voice.

'Mr Tyrone!' the voice said. It sounded like the voice of a machine. Tris could barely understand a word of it.

'I suppose they think they've sneaked up on me without being noticed,' Orson said. 'Okay, Monsieur. Go to the door. Hey, sweetie ... you can go, too.'

Winola let out a deep groaning sigh. Hearing this sound, Tris knew for certain she had just been lying there, escaping from Orson in the only way she could, probably waiting for him to roll over, poisoned.

'Oh, come off it!' Orson exclaimed, sounding irritated. 'I know you've been putting it on. Very clever! Why wouldn't you say one kind word? Just one. The only kind word I've had is from Monsieur, here.'

Winola scrambled to her feet. She looked at her father, but remained silent.

'Out you go and mingle with the Armed Offenders' Squad,' Orson said.

'Yes, but . . .' Tris said, hesitating. The knocking came on the door again. It sounded relaxed, as if there were no great hurry over anything.

'Don't . . .' Tris began, looking at Orson for the last time.

Winola came up behind him, in no hurry, either. She moved calmly, almost casually, pushing Tris out first, then shutting the door behind her. 'Don't!' commanded Tris through the crack in the closing door, and saw Orson, still smiling, but slumping down in his chair. The door clicked shut. Tris thought he heard Winola's teeth chatter slightly, but then it might have been his own.

The street light outside flooded the hall with a ghostly light. Tris stopped short, seizing Winola's arm so that she stopped too, and looked questioningly at him.

'Did you poison that coffee?' Tris whispered.

'Come on!' she muttered.

'Did you, though?'

'It was only my antihistamine,' she hissed. 'I thought it might put him to sleep. Come on.'

'He might . . . you know . . . kill himself,' said Tris.

'He didn't last time,' Winola said.

She turned a key, and opened the door.

The man standing on the step, raising his hand to knock at the door for a third time, was Randall Catt.

He was wearing his old lumber jacket, but Tris could see one side of it was padded out, probably with bandages. He had a piece of plaster over one eye.

'I thought you were dead,' Tris managed to say. 'I thought . . .' He could not go on.

'Catts always fall on their feet,' said Randall. He kneeled down on the doorstep.

'Tris, you're the treasure of my life,' he said quickly. 'You know that, don't you?'

'Yes,' said Tris, because it was short to say, and besides, he knew it was true. Out in the street, beyond Randall, stood police cars, and beyond them, a television van. There were armed men in the tiny garden to the right and left of the door. An old couple in their dressing-gowns were being helped into one of the cars. The noises that had sounded so muffled in the house were sharp and distinct out here, several voices talking at once, the sound of a radio voice giving instructions, and beyond all this the murmur of indifferent traffic for, after all, it was not so late, and all around them was the Saturday night of the city.

'Just walk over to the police cars there,' Randall instructed Tris and Winola. 'Tell them everything they need to know. I'm going into the house to talk to Orson – if he'll let me.'

'He's in there,' Winola said. 'Trying to stay awake.'

'He might kill himself,' Tris told Randall. 'He's thinking of it.'

'Once he sees that I'm well and strong he might change his mind,' said Randall gently. 'Off you go, kids! See you soon.'

Tris hesitated.

'Go on!' repeated Randall. 'I know what I'm doing. I met Orson once or twice years ago. We're old friends, and besides . . . I'm good at this.'

As Tris went out of Dearie's house, Randall went into it.

People came towards them, anxious to surround them and bring them into the safety zone, but Tris suddenly saw Victoria waiting in the shadows. It seemed quite natural for him to run to her, for her to hug him, and for him to hug her back, as policemen crowded round them.

'Oh, thank you! Thank you!' she was saying, though he didn't quite know who she was saying thank you to. 'Oh, Tris!' She was crying and, unlike Winola, Tris had plenty of tears left for when he needed them. It seemed strange, though, to need them when everything was turning out all right. A policewoman put her arm around Winola, guiding her in behind the van, and within a moment they were as safe as it was possible to be in a dangerous world.

CHAPTER FIFTEEN

———— · ————

'I'm coming to your place,' Sylvia said, and then waited to be invited, just as she had a week earlier.

Tris hesitated, half expecting the yellow Lotus to glide up beside them once more, with Orson leaning on the door, looking at them through his dark glasses and asking the way to Featherstonehaugh Children's Home. But the road was empty.

'Tomorrow!' he said. 'Come tomorrow.'

Sylvia was taken aback at getting a proper invitation. She glanced suspiciously at Tris in case he was joking.

'Promise!' she commanded him.

'Promise! We'll have something to eat by then,' said Tris.

'Will I have to whisper and tiptoe?' she asked, booming as if they were calling from hilltop to hilltop.

'Not tomorrow,' said Tris.

'Okay,' Sylvia agreed. 'It's a date.' She began walking up the hill, then stopped and looked down at him.

'I'm not just coming because of getting something to eat,' she called. 'I'm being *friendly*.'

'We've got other visitors today,' Tris called back. 'That Mrs Emanuell!'

'Yes, and some other people too! Come tomorrow. Promise.'

'Promise!' she repeated, turning her back on him as she did so, so that the sound of the word, though not its sense, drifted up into the leaves.

Tris went on walking home. It was hard to believe that he was back doing what he usually did, just as if nothing had happened. Yet here he was and here was the road, and everything was just as it had always been.

Not quite as it had always been, though. Guy and Brian had said their usual mocking things all day, but at the same time they had looked at him differently, respecting his fearsome adventure and his survival, and boasting of the fact that they had been sprayed with gravel by the Lotus. On the way home Guy had let him have a turn on his ten-speed.

But now that Sylvia had climbed up between the gum trees on her hill, Tris found he was completely alone. No Selsey Firebone walked through him or talked through him any more. When Tris closed his eyes and tried to get in touch with Selsey, it was like climbing a stair to a room where there had always been someone waiting, and then finding it empty. The imaginary door was open, the imaginary room was filled with sunlight and friendly space, the windows were flung wide, letting in a warm breeze, but there was no one in the room at all.

Still, Tris did not feel lonely. He walked on, up and over the hill, barely glancing at the Featherstonehaugh Children's Home chimneys. When he came to the place where he had always turned off to edge along between the scrub and the steel-mesh fence, he stayed on the road. It was not just that he missed the thought of Cecily Winola Tyrone, not just that he did not want to see the hollow where she had once squeezed under the fence. It was that he now no longer felt any need to hide from anything. All that was over and done with. *Featherstonehaugh Children's Home*, said the notice by the gate. Tris paused and looked at it and wondered how it was that a word spelt like Featherstonehaugh could ever be pronounced 'Fanshaw'. Once, the idea of it had bothered him. Once, it had seemed the world was making fun of him. Now, he began to think it was a *sign* (he heard the word spoken in Winola's ominous voice), a sign that the world was far more mysterious than he had ever imagined it could be. Worrying too much over the mystery was a way of shutting it out. What you had to do was recognize it and let it soak into you, thinking about it in a secret way. The notice was a sly joke just to *remind* you.

The council roadman, who filled the pot holes and put gravel on icy corners in the winter so that cars would not slide, had been by in his grass-clipping chariot. The ditch was filled with long, fading stems. But even if it had still been an overgrown green tunnel Tris would not have climbed along it any more. Walking openly uphill beside the ditch he wondered how it was that now, after a really frightening thing had happened, he felt that he did not have to hide. A voice spoke in his head, spoke in the sunny room with the open windows, but it was not Selsey Firebone speaking. It was Winola, the friendly princess. She said the same thing that she had written to him from her new foster home the night before.

'Perhaps you knew the future,' she was saying in her story-telling way. 'Perhaps you knew something was going to happen, and now it has you don't have to worry about it any more.'

Tris preferred to think that he had suddenly become braver.

He stopped and looked around.

'Okay! Come and get me!' he suddenly shouted to his ancient fears. The shout went echoing in all directions, up to the hilltops, out towards the end of the diving man. Tris waited in the sunny autumn silence but no fears answered his challenge.

Yet, as he climbed the second hill, he saw someone was coming to get him. He knew at once it was his father, but his father changed in some way. As they walked towards one another, smiling, Tris stared at him, trying to work out just what the change was. Randall began talking almost at once, shouting down the hill to him.

'I was going to meet you after school,' he cried, 'but I forgot the time.'

They moved towards each other, Tris climbing up, Randall coming down.

'Just like you!' Tris shouted back.

Then they met. In the back of his mind Tris now carried for ever a memory of the space in front of Dearie's house, filled with people. The mixed light from the street lamp and the police van had turned everyone but Winola and Victoria into aliens. There were armed men around the house, and in the dark buildings behind him as well.

'Don't worry about Randall,' Victoria had whispered. 'He knows what he's doing.' Tris saw in her face that, in spite of her brave words, she was worried about Randall herself.

'He'll be okay!' Tris whispered back, glad to hug and comfort her. 'He's *ace* at counselling.'

At last the door, with its panels of stained glass, opened slowly and Randall came out, carrying the gun under his right arm, his left hand on Orson's shoulder. Selsey Firebone was there, alive in the outside world, not in Orson, the man with the gun and the car, but partly in Cissy Tyrone who had rechristened herself Winola, partly in Randall, and perhaps even in Tris himself, dissolved into his blood for ever. Remembering this, Tris suddenly realized why Randall looked so strange.

'Hey!' he cried. 'You've cut your hair!'

Randall nodded, perhaps a little sadly.

'I have to grow up sometime, I suppose,' he said. 'Anything interesting happen at school today?'

Tris thought carefully. He longed to tell Randall something just to please him, but the more he thought about the day the more it seemed as if nothing had happened that was in the least worth telling about.

'Nothing!' he said at last.

'Thank goodness!' Randall exclaimed. 'Good old, safe old nothing!'

They walked through the splintered remains of the gate.

'I collected the mail, and guess what?' Randall said.

'More warnings about gorse?' suggested Tris.

'No! Something for you.' Randall took a letter from the pocket of his overalls and held it out to Tris. It was a thick white envelope with dashing black writing across it. In the top corner were Australian stamps.

'From her?' asked Tris. He couldn't believe it. In a way he had never really believed that a letter would ever come, even though he had looked for one for so long. Now, immediately he had stopped thinking about it, a letter had arrived.

'That's her handwriting,' said Randall.

'She's just writing because of what happened,' Tris exclaimed.

'Wake up,' said Randall. 'That's from Sydney. Your mum couldn't possibly have known what's been going on here.'

'It might have been on television!' Tris said. Other

people had seen him on television coming out of Dearie's house.

'They've got too many dramas of their own over there,' Randall said. 'She wrote because she had something to say to you.'

Tris put the envelope carefully into his pack.

'Aren't you going to read it?' Randall asked, looking inquisitive.

'I'll read it later,' Tris answered.

'It might be an invitation to visit her in Sydney,' Randall suggested. 'If it is . . .'

'Not counselling!' cried Tris. 'I don't need to be counselled.'

'No.' Randall sounded a little hurt. 'All right, then! Listen to my news. Victoria gave me a lift into town this morning, and I went to see Malley & Pearson.' Malley & Pearson were the landscape gardening firm he did part-time work for. 'They've offered me a full-time job, and I don't think I'd better turn it down. You should never turn down the magic chance at the right time.'

Odd memories darted in and out, nibbling at the edges of Tris's thoughts. For instance, here, at the place they were walking past so cheerfully, Orson had once stood looking back towards Featherstonehaugh Children's Home through his binoculars. Tris marched on, ignoring the possible ghost. Orson was 'being looked after', Randall had said. 'We'll just have to see what happens. There are all sorts of ways of being unhappy.' He was in a place in another city, a cross between a prison and a hospital.

'You mean you're getting a proper job?' Tris asked, trying to forget Orson.

'Yes,' said Randall.

The whole of the diving man shivered around Tris, the tussocks, gorse, pine trees, the lumpy shoulders and the dissolving hands that held his house so securely above the sea. Overhead, the hawk hung, waiting, in the air. Even the indifferent geese down on the tide-line seemed to raise their heads, waiting. The labyrinth of underrunners writhed a little below Tris's feet.

'We're not going to have to *move* from here, are we?' he cried, panic-stricken. 'I don't want to live anywhere else.'

'Neither do I,' said Randall. 'But it deserves better care . . . a better caretaker. It's eroding all the time. Right this minute it's being eaten away. You know, I love the idea of being the strong, self-sufficient Kiwi joker, but let's face it, I'm just not good enough at it. I've known that for a long time, really.'

'Are we going away?' Tris cried.

'Lord, no!' Randall replied. 'It's home. Well, isn't it?' he asked rather shyly. Tris nodded violently. 'Well, starting from the week after next, I'll work at what I'm good at and get other people who are good at fencing and fixing generators and so on to do some of the work here for me.'

They walked along the winding track, moving

from one side of the peninsula to the other, and things looked familiar, just as they always did, yet for ever new. Today everything sparkled. The first thin film of high-tide water had barely covered the mud and sand below. The reflections of the hills had an odd, mottled look to them because the casts of thousands of crabs who lived in the mud had not yet been covered over. Two minutes more, two long ripples later, this little roughness would vanish until the moon began pulling the water back again.

'Dad,' said Tris. 'If you wanted to marry Victoria I wouldn't mind.'

'Ah,' said his father. 'But it's not just a matter of getting your permission. I have to get hers.'

'Doesn't she want to marry you?' asked Tris, astonished.

'She's thinking it over,' said Randall. 'I haven't got a great track record in some ways. Mind you, she can see that I'm a wonderful father. And don't you forget it!'

They walked on in silence. The track twisted, taking them to the other side of the peninsula.

'The thing is I'll have to go in and out,' said Randall, 'just like the tide. And I'll need something the sea doesn't need. I'll need a car. And I'll need someone who knows about cars to give me good advice.'

'A car!' cried Tris. Last week this would have made him shine with happiness. This week it was good news, too, but in a different way. 'I'll be able to learn to drive. What sort?'

'You suggest something!' said Randall. 'Not a Fiat X19. And not a Lotus Elan!'

As they came down towards the house Tris saw two cars were already waiting there. One was Victoria's Volkswagen, the other a strange car, a new one . . . a Mazda.

'You've got a visitor,' said Randall, and as he spoke Winola suddenly appeared in the doorway.

She looked even thinner than Tris remembered her. She was wearing new blue jeans but not a very good brand. Her left hand was taped around with plaster. Her right one was still bandaged.

'Wounded people get extra cake,' said Randall.

'Yeah! We need building up,' agreed Winola.

'Is there cake?' asked Tris.

'I made one specially,' Randall told him.

'I'm visiting,' Winola pointed out. 'Visiting properly. Not being Elaine Thingummy.'

In the pole house Victoria was talking to Mrs Forbes, the foster mother with whom Winola had been placed three days earlier. She seemed a pleasant, kind woman who did not mind Rosie making a bed for Bombom in a long patchwork bag she had brought with her to hold her knitting. The knitting was spread around her feet. Bombom looked happy in a plaintive, stretched-out way.

'Ratty!' cried Rosie. 'Cake for Ratty!'

Winola and Tris were each given a slab of Randall's dense fruitcake. There were no underrunners in Randall's cookery. Armed with provisions, they set out together on to the hills. Once they were away from the house, Winola looked at him curiously.

'That was a great plan of yours,' she said.

'What was?' asked Tris.

'Crying, so that Orson let us go,' she said. 'Was it you or Selsey Firebone?'

'It wasn't a plan,' Tris confessed awkwardly. 'I just did.'

'I can't cry,' Winola said. 'He got me out of the habit.'

'I suddenly felt sorry for him,' Tris said. 'I don't know why. He looked sort of lonely.'

'It's his own fault if he was lonely,' Winola murmured, but she gave Tris a look of puzzled respect. Tris could not understand just why he had felt so sorry for terrible Orson.

'His mother used to read him *The Wind in the Willows*,' he said vaguely. It didn't seem much of a reason when you said it aloud to someone like Winola. Tris changed the subject.

'I think my dad and Victoria are going to get married,' he told her, suddenly bursting with the proposition he had to put to her – something he had been working out continually for the past three days.

'I think so too,' Winola agreed. 'They behave like it – always touching hands and saying each other's names and that. You know how people do. They try to make it look as if they were doing it by accident.'

'The thing is,' Tris said, 'if they get married we'll

be a proper family, and we'll be allowed to adopt you, and you can come and live here. Not in an underrunner. In the house!'

Winola was walking a few steps ahead of him, pushing uphill, and she did not stop.

'I'm not one of those too-big kittens that someone's dumped!' she exclaimed indignantly.

'I know,' Tris said quickly. 'But you fit in here now.'

Winola stopped and blew her nose on a clean handkerchief.

'Well, the thing is,' she said at last, 'it won't work. I've already got a mother. I'll go back home before too long.'

'Back to *that* house?' Tris couldn't believe it.

'Well, it's all we've got,' said Winola. 'And then there's Damon! Though he'll probably shack up with his mates when he gets out.'

It had never occurred to Tris that Winola might turn down his offer. It had seemed such an inevitable end to their adventure – the proper end for a story. He felt numb with disappointment.

'I don't want you just to be another cat,' he cried. 'I want you to be a sister and to be safe.'

'You don't have to worry about me,' said Winola. 'And you know why?' She suddenly turned and stood over him, tall and bony, her grey eyes shining into his. 'Because I'm really tough!' she said. 'I know that! I'm not crazy like Dearie or Orson or Damon, and I'm not dead like Tod. I only have to hang on a bit longer and I'll be grown up.'

'What will you do then, though?' asked Tris.

She shrugged. 'I don't know yet,' she said. 'Something!'

Tris snatched at a tall tussock discontentedly. He wanted things tied up, a truly happy ending. Something like a tiny hot wire burned across his palm. The tussock had cut him.

'You have to have food to eat,' he grumbled. 'You have to have money!'

'I'll get some,' said Winola, 'and I'll come to visit you for cake. Is your hand bleeding?'

'It's nothing!' said Tris.

'Blood should not fall in vain. There's a spirit in it,' Winola said, tearing the plaster from her own left hand, using her teeth. 'Hang on a moment!' She flexed her fingers, opening the old cuts and squeezing blood from the parallel lines that ran along her palm.

'Only a few drops!' she said. 'That's enough, though! It'll do.'

She held out her hand. Tris took it as he knew he must.

'I vow you to be my blood brother,' she said. 'Not just a sibling, like it says in the reports. You know . . . "The subject has two male siblings . . ." A *blood* brother! Now, you say it to me.'

'I vow you to be my blood sister,' Tris said. Winola smiled and let his hand go. Then she licked the blood away, Tris's as well as her own.

'I'm going to gallop!' she said. And off she went, galloping, galloping down the slope. Tris watched her go. Putting his hand into his pocket to find his own handkerchief he found his mother's letter, still waiting to be read. He stood there under the wide sky, and opened it slowly, staining the white envelope as he did so.

'*Dearest Tristram,*' he read. '*This must be the hardest letter I have ever written in all my life. I have been meaning to write it for the last two years, but I have kept on putting it off, because I have so much to be sorry for, and I hate saying I am sorry to anyone . . .*'

Winola frisked and galloped away on her own. Tris glanced hastily down towards the bottom of the letter.

'*. . . I do want to promise you that nothing that has happened was your fault . . .*' he read.

'Big deal!' he heard Winola say, almost as if she were speaking in his ear.

The letter was too important to read while so much else was going on. In a way, at that moment, it was more important, more urgent, to gallop in the sun, to look up into the sky where hawks and larks flew, or at trees growing out of the body of the diving man, or down on to the tide-lines where the geese lived their private, foraging lives, crying out warnings when shadows moved over them.

'Hey, blood brother! Are you coming?' called Winola impatiently.

Tris wanted to give some cry – half a war cry and half a secret password that only Winola would recognize. He took a breath but didn't know what it should be. Then suddenly he knew for sure.

'Fanshaw! Fanshaw! Fanshaw!' he shouted, charging down the slope.

Winola laughed aloud.

'Fanshaw! Fanshaw! Fanshaw!' she yelled back to him.

Everything around them was still, yet moving within its own stillness. The diving man dived, the underrunners opened grassy lips, crying silently into space, the hovering hawks hung there watching and waiting for prey. Tris galloped, flinging out his arms, breathing in. Winola galloped ahead of him. And in a way they were not one but two Selsey Firebones, set free for the moment to race under the open sky.